OPERATION MISTLETOE

OPERATION MISTLETOE

OPERATION ROMANCE BOOK 1

ELIZABETH MADDREY

Scripture quoted by permission. Quotations designated (NIV) are from THE HOLY BIBLE: NEW INTERNATIONAL VERSION®. NIV®. Copyright © 1973, 1978, 1984 by Biblica. All rights reserved worldwide.

Cover design by Elizabeth Maddrey.

Cover art photos ©iStockphoto.com/heather_mcgrath, ©iStockphoto.-com/smiltena used by permission.

Published in the United States of America by Elizabeth Maddrey. www.ElizabethMaddrey.com

1

Tori Spencer slammed down a stack of file folders and stood. Her chair shot back and smacked into the wall. If steam wasn't coming out of her ears, it should be. Who, exactly, did Ryan Morrison think he was? She yanked at the bottom edge of her blazer and, teeth clenched, strode through the maze of low-walled cubicles to the offices that lined the windows. She gave a cursory rap on the open door and crossed her arms.

Ryan looked up from his computer and slid his glasses down his nose. "Victoria?"

"The Christmas light feature?"

"What about it?" Ryan took off his glasses and laid them on his desk before gesturing to a chair.

"I don't do fluff pieces. You know that. That's not what I was hired for. Can't someone else do this? Jeri? An intern?" Tori crossed the room but didn't sit. Once he agreed with her and apologized for his momentary lapse, she was leaving.

He pinched the bridge of his nose. "Shut the door and sit down."

She furrowed her brow. The tone of his voice bordered on ominous. Huffing out a breath, she did as instructed.

"Look. This isn't a fluff piece. It's one of the most read articles during this season. Add in the fact that we're doing a feature spread on one of the guys, Gabriel Robertson." Ryan pushed papers around on his desk until he unearthed a stack of orange sticky notes. He paged through them and finally pulled one off, offering it to her. "Here's his contact info. He takes all the proceeds from his display and uses them to send Christmas to the troops deployed overseas. It's a good special interest angle and is something a little different than the retreads we usually end up with this time of year."

Gabe Robertson...no way. There was absolutely no way. Not like her college crush on him still lingered. But still. Tori shook her head, sending her ponytail swinging violently. "So get someone else to do it and give me something that's worth my time. You *know* I'm a better journalist than this..."

"Can it, Tori. You and I both know why you're working here instead of for a major paper doing exposes on politicians on Capitol Hill. So take your assignment, make some calls, set up appointments, and get me my feature." Ryan's fist slammed down on his desk, sharpened pencils rattling in the mug where he kept them.

Her chest constricted and she fought to keep her face straight. "Do I at least get a photographer?"

Ryan pursed his lips and stared at her. The old-fashioned school clock ticked loudly from its position on the wall. "You can check out a camera. I don't have anyone free right now, but if you get me a good feature with decent snaps of your own, maybe I'll send someone out for follow up pics."

Heat washed over her. Now she was a reporter *and* a photographer? What was next? Doing her own editing? Nah. He'd never let a chance to wield his red pencil slip by. "Fine."

"Good." When she didn't move, Ryan arched an eyebrow. "Was there something else?"

Tori stifled a groan. The set of Ryan's mouth had her shaking her head as she stood instead of asking for a different assignment one more time. He was serious. Perfect. Just. Perfect.

"All right then. Close the door on your way out."

TWENTY-FOUR MORE DAYS until the other shoe—whatever that ended up being—dropped. Tori kicked her three-inch heels toward the closet. They bounced across the carpet and landed right in front of the door to the bathroom. Where she'd probably step on them in the middle of the night and break something. Grumbling under her breath, she crossed the room and grabbed the shoes, lining them neatly next to the sixteen other pairs of professional-with-just-a-hint-of-sexy heels she owned. Her lips curved as her gaze roamed over the gleaming, supple leather. Why couldn't all of life be as simple and full of variety as shoes?

"Oh, no you don't, Woodsie." Tori scooped up her Ragdoll/Maine-Coon mix and ruffled his ears. "You know you're not allowed in the closet. Where's Bernie? Already sitting by his bowl, waiting for dinner, right?"

The cat gave a sullen *prrow* as she pulled the closet door closed and headed toward the kitchen. She paused to scoop out dry cat food before setting Woodsie down by his bowl. "Bernie, dinner."

Her other, nearly identical, cat trotted into the kitchen, his gravelly voice giving her an animated rundown of his various feline complaints. She smiled and ran a hand from his head to tail after he hopped up and began to eat.

Tori's cell buzzed on the counter. Her mother's cheerful face lit up the display and Tori's heart sank. The perfect cap to a terrible day. "Hey, Mom."

"Tori, honey, how are you? You didn't call on Sunday like you usually do and now it's Tuesday. I've been so worried. What's going on?"

She moved into the living room and sank into the couch. "Nothing, Mom. You know how the weekends get, and then yesterday I had a major deadline, so I was rushing to get my article finished. I'd planned to call you later tonight. What's up?"

Her mother gave a breathy sigh. "Well, I was wondering if you'd figured out your Christmas plans yet?"

"You know I don't do Christmas, Mom." Every year they had the same conversation. When was Mom going to get the idea?

"Oh, please. Are you still going on about your supposed Christmas curse?"

Supposed? "Ten years, Mom. It's been ten years of disaster without fail."

"That simply isn't possible. What was wrong with Christmas when you were sixteen?"

Tori scoffed. "You're not serious."

"Of course I am. Tell me."

Here we go. "Let's see, Christmas of 1989, Grandma died. At our house, on Christmas Eve. Do you not remember her having a heart attack at the table?"

"Oh, right. Your father's mom. She never liked me. Plus she was old. I hardly see that as a disaster, though I suppose I'll concede that it took the shine off the holiday that year. Still, it isn't as if someone died every year."

"No, that's true. The next year, you and Dad announced that you were getting a divorce. On Christmas Eve. At the dinner table."

"Hmm. Perhaps we should have timed that better. But the year after that, you got a car for Christmas."

Tori shook her head. "As Dad's attempt at softening the news that he was getting married. The year after that, his wife had a baby and they named her Victoria, never thinking that maybe, just maybe, Dad's first daughter with that name might be annoyed by that."

"Your father has never had a lot of empathy, dear. I'm sure he just went along with whatever that woman wanted."

Tori switched the phone to her other ear and patted her lap. Woodsie leapt onto the couch and arranged himself half-on, half-off her leg. "The year I turned twenty, you took me skiing for a week and I broke my leg. The year after that, you used your Christmas card to announce your elopement with a man scarcely four years older than I am."

"I don't see why you insist on categorizing my happiness as a disaster. Honestly, Tori, not everything is about you. You realize that, right?"

She covered her face with her hands and started counting silently. When it came to her parents, not only wasn't everything about her, nothing was. "Of course. But at least Dad introduced me to my step-mother before he up and married her."

Her mother's aggrieved sigh blew through the phone speaker into her ear. "And look how well that worked out for him. You refused to go to the wedding. So it's not like I didn't have a precedent. Whatever. I was hoping that you had some plans with friends this year so you wouldn't have an excuse to be mad at me, but since it seems like no matter what I do, I'm going to be the one at fault, I'll just tell you that Zane and I are headed to the Caymans tomorrow and we're planning to spend a month, maybe two, sailing the Caribbean. So if you were planning to visit, you'll need to figure something else out. Maybe your father and that woman have room for you. Although, the way she keeps popping out kids, that might not be a possibility."

Tori swallowed the lump in her throat. "He let me know in

October that they're taking their family on a cruise over Christmas."

"And he's not taking you? You're his family too. I ought to—"

"Don't worry about it, Mom. Go have fun on your sailboat with Zane. Thanks for letting me know. Send me a postcard, okay?" Tori's head dropped back and she stared at the ceiling. Dad had invited her along, but she hadn't wanted to leave Mom alone. Zane usually planned guy weekends with his friends over the holidays. Maybe now that he was in his thirties his friends were settling down and he'd realized that he needed to spend time with his wife if he wanted to keep her.

"I can talk to Zane, see if there's room for you to tag along?"

Her mom's conciliatory tone made her smile. "No. That wouldn't be fun for anyone. Besides, I don't have the flexibility in my job to work from a boat like Zane and you do. Don't worry about me. I'll be fine. Love you."

Tori ended the call and dropped her phone on the cushion, the remainder of her Christmas disasters flitting through her mind. At twenty-two, her mom had miscarried on Christmas Eve and Tori had been the one to rush her to the hospital and stay with her through an emergency hysterectomy and the ensuing recovery. At twenty-three, she'd awakened Christmas morning to smoke alarms blaring because one of the upstairs apartments had decided to have a vintage Christmas theme, complete with real candles on a real tree. Everyone got out of the building without incident, but between the fire, smoke, and water damage, Tori had endured a total loss, causing her insurance rates to skyrocket. Christmas twenty-four was the year she thought she'd been dressing up for a marriage proposal and had ended up dumped instead by a chicken-livered boyfriend who had thought dining at the Ritz would keep her from making a scene. Last year she'd woken up Christmas morning with a one hundred two degree fever and nearly ended up in the hospital since there hadn't been anyone to help take care of her and make sure she stayed hydrated. This year she already had three disasters in the making, though not spending time with either of her parents and their new families wasn't necessarily a bad thing. But a feature on former college crush Gabe "The Babe" Robertson? That had disaster written all over it.

Bernie hopped up into her lap and began to knead her leg. She rubbed his head. "Christmas is for the birds, boys."

2

Gabe rubbed his hands together, as much in anticipation as to stave off the chill. The first weekend of December—opening night for the third-annual Winter Wonderland. He'd started pulling boxes out of the old barn during the week of Halloween. Setup, starting at the back of his property and moving forward through the nearly five acres, had taken every spare minute since.

"Ready?" His friend and business partner, Jake, hooked his thumbs into his pockets and crossed from his truck to the porch where Gabe stood.

"Think so. I did a walk-through last night, everything looks like it's working. The maps came today, and I saw that the town blocked off some extra parking along the street in front, so we should be good to go. Hear anything from Rick lately?"

Jake shrugged. "Just the usual check-in. I'm still surprised he was okay with staying in Germany for Christmas. Doesn't he have a sister back here?"

"He has a sister, but I think her husband's military and they're deployed right now. Coming back in February maybe?

So I'm guessing he'll want some vacation time then. Things are going smoothly enough that you can stay stateside if you want."

"Nah. I'll head back in January like we planned. Things work better with me and Rick over there, boots on the ground if you will, and you handling business here. Besides, neither of us wants to take on all those meetings with the brass at the Pentagon. You just keep doing what you're doing."

Gabe chuckled. "All right, thought I'd offer. Come on, I'll show you your post. Entrance is free, with a suggested five dollar donation per family, but the skating rink and snacks are all paid."

"I know this, man. You've been over it six times." Jake modulated his voice to one of a radio announcer. "All proceeds go to Operation Mistletoe, a locally-based non-profit organization committed to taking holiday gifts to the men and women serving overseas as well as supplying needed encouragement throughout the year."

Gabe punched Jake's arm.

"Ow. What?"

"There's no need to be obnoxious."

"Right. You're hovering like a mother hen. I've got this. Go...warm up cocoa or something."

Checking on the hot chocolate wasn't a bad idea. People would start arriving any minute. The sun was nearly set and the twinkling white lights lining the front driveway were a welcoming beacon of Christmas cheer. "All right. If someone from the NoVa Tribune comes, hit me on the walkie and I'll come running. The editor promised to do a feature on me this year. I'm hoping we can double what we donated last year."

Jake shook his head and made a shooing motion as a couple, holding hands, strolled up the driveway while two kids skipped around them in circles, chattering.

Gabe waited until Jake started in on his spiel before ducking through the cordoned off area around St. Nicholas square—an area dedicated to light displays featuring Santa in all his various forms. He crossed Grinch Gulch, skirted around Ralphie's Retreat, his lips twitching as he passed the leg lamp centerpiece, and finally arrived at the main attraction. The live Nativity, staffed by volunteers from his church, was in place. Donkeys munched contentedly on hay and sheep milled in their pen. A quick check confirmed the feed pails were full of pellets for kids to grab and offer to the docile creatures.

He waved to the cast. "Couple of people are already here. Don't hesitate to take a break when you need one though, just put the mannequins in place as needed."

They murmured assent as Gabe unlocked the front window of the snack bar located across the small clearing. There were picnic tables, as well as some single chairs and rockers, scattered around. He wanted people to be comfortable so they'd take the time to watch the Nativity or listen to the various choirs that would be singing carols.

"You ready in here, Doris?"

His next-door neighbor, owner of the majority of the livestock keeping Baby Jesus company, poked her head out of the tiny refrigerator and nodded, her silvery-grey curls bouncing. "Just finished checking on the supplies. We're all set. Don's on his way over as soon as he's home from work, which should be any minute. You sure having a live Santa doesn't conflict with that out there?"

"I'm sure. Saint Nicholas is a historical figure and that's what I highlight on the map. Generosity and giving to those in need in the name of Christ is what this is all about. Between the Nativity and the candy cane story, plus avoiding any of the secular Christmas songs, I think we're pretty clear on who we're saying is the reason for the season."

Doris pursed her lips and gave a slow nod. "All right. If you're sure."

"You holler if you need anything, okay?"

"I will. When's the choir showing up?"

Gabe frowned and glanced at the bulky, military-style watch on his wrist. "They should be here. I guess that's the next thing I need to figure out."

He wound his way through the other half of the lights, checking that the paths were clearly marked and no bulbs were out on his way back to the house. He didn't have the contact information for the opening night music on his phone. He slapped Jake on the back as he passed by. "No reporter yet?"

"Not one who's said anything about it." Jake grinned at a family who stuffed a wad of cash into the donation bucket as they took a map.

With a nod, Gabe strode the rest of the way to the house, taking the porch steps two at a time. The first night always had hiccups. It was the nature of any big operation, but Ryan had promised an interview or some sort of feature that went beyond a simple listing with all the other light displays out there. This one mattered—both for its focus on the real reason for Christmas and for all the good they could do for the men and women serving overseas. It was hard enough being away from home during the holidays, but to miss out on the chance to know that their Savior had been born? Not if he could do anything about that.

The red light on his house phone was blinking. He hit play on the message and started digging through the pile of papers on his desk for the choir schedule and contact information he'd printed out. His shoulders fell as the choir director's voice spilled into the room. Of course their bus had gotten a flat tire. Why wouldn't it? He blew out a breath. Maybe it was good that reporter hadn't shown up after all.

GABE TOOK a long drink of coffee as he paged through the weekend edition of the local paper. Why hadn't Ryan followed through with his promise? There was still tonight, but that would mean the story would run when? The tiny paper didn't publish anything on Sunday. That made sense. No point trying to compete with the big presses on their most subscribed day. But still. He found the Holiday Calendar. At least his listing was there...along with about twenty others. He needed that feature to stand out in the crowd.

There was a brisk knock at the door. Coffee mug in hand, Gabe rose to answer it. It had to be Doris and Dan stopping by to chat about last night. Maybe she'd have some of those cherry turnovers she made. His mouth watered. He could almost taste the tart cherries and sweet, flaky pastry. He opened the door and frowned. The beautiful young woman on his porch was definitely *not* Doris.

"Can I help you?" He studied the tidy black pantsuit and red hair pulled back into an efficient tail. Everything about her screamed "no nonsense," and yet there was enough there to pique a man's interest. And it had been entirely too long since he'd let himself be interested.

A sharp smile formed on her lips and her hand jutted out. "Good morning, Mr. Robertson. I'm Victoria Spencer from the *NoVa Tribune*. Do you have a few minutes? I'd like to talk to you about your light display."

Gabe bristled, his interest dimming, as he shook her hand, her soft skin a contrast to her firm grip. Did she have any idea the time and effort that went into this? "I expected you last night. It doesn't give quite the same impression in the daylight."

"Ah, well...I got held up on another story." Pink tinged her cheeks as her eyebrows winged up. "Is now a bad time?"

He sighed and pushed the door open wider. "No, it's fine. Come on in. Can I get you a cup of coffee?"

3

Tori let her gaze roam. Anything to avoid focusing on the fact that Gabe had only gotten better looking as he'd aged. He'd worked out in college like the rest of the frat boys. But now? He was chiseled. Not even the flannel shirt he wore unbuttoned over his thermal Henley could hide that. He wore his black hair close-cropped now, almost a military style. It suited him, just like the floppier, devil-may-care haircut of college had. Was it possible for him to look bad? She followed him through the casual-yet-elegant living room into the state-of-the-art kitchen. Did he cook? He must, or why would he have this kind of setup? The house was old enough that a kitchen like this had been put in recently. Maybe the previous owners? The party-boy she'd crushed on in college had never indicated any sort of prowess with pots and pans.

Gabe pulled a chair out from the octagonal pine table nestled in a bay window. "Cream and sugar?"

"Just black is fine." She shrugged out of her coat, sat, and pulled a small voice recorder out of her purse. "You don't mind if I record this? It makes doing the story easier."

He shrugged, glancing over as he poured coffee from a French press. "Sure, that's fine."

Tori watched him, his casual, easy manner sending a familiar frisson through her. Did he recognize her? He didn't give any indication that he did. They hadn't been friends, though they'd shared a few general education classes and had pleasant conversations when he hadn't been surrounded by his frat buddies. Not the time for those sorts of thoughts. She sipped the coffee he set in front of her and smiled. "That's good."

"You sound surprised." He leaned back in his chair and lifted his own mug to his lips.

"I guess I am. The military isn't known for their coffee. From the background info my editor gave me, you spend a lot of time overseas, working with the troops. I guess I assumed their brewing techniques would rub off."

He chuckled. "I can probably scare up a dirty sock for you to dip in your cup if you need that experience to round out the interview."

"No. No, that won't be necessary." He'd always had a clever tongue. Though it didn't seem as sharp now. Was that a change in him or in her? "Why don't we get started? Why a Christmas light show? Why not just make a donation from your company to Operation Mistletoe?"

Gabe blinked. "Wow. We do, actually, make a donation from the company. But Operation Mistletoe is a fantastic cause, and it's not one most people know about. So this gives folks a way to participate while enjoying a family outing that they'd probably be taking anyway."

"And how do you split the proceeds?"

"What do you mean?" Gabe frowned as he leaned forward, bracing his arms on the table.

Tori gestured broadly with one hand. "All those lights, employees, choirs? It has to cost something. Surely you don't expect people to believe that you aren't reimbursed for that? And why shouldn't you be? So how much goes to cover expenses? Is it a percentage? A flat amount?"

"Not a cent." Gabe pushed back from the table. "But since I can see you don't believe me, we're done here. Let me show you out. Don't forget your coat."

"There's no reason to get huffy, Mr. Robertson. If you have nothing to hide, then simply answering the questions..."

The muscles in his jaw bunched, but his lips remained pressed firmly together. His chest rose as he took a deep breath, nostrils flaring as he exhaled. "Have a nice day, Ms. Spencer."

Fine. She didn't want to do this story anyway. Tori punched the stop button on her recorder, tucked it back in her purse as she stood, and grabbed her jacket from the back of the chair. "I still don't..."

Gabe raised one hand and gave one sharp shake of his head. "This way."

"I NEED copy for the feature on Robertson's Christmas display." Ryan leaned against Tori's cube wall. "When will you have it ready?"

Tori frowned and swiveled to face him. "I sent you the light display piece two hours ago."

"Yeah, got it. It's not great, mind you, but it'll flesh out the calendar page some. But you'll recall we're—by which I mean you're—also doing a feature on Robertson and the Operation Mistletoe fundraiser." Ryan nodded toward her computer monitor. "Is that it?"

"Not really." Tori clicked the minimize bar. It was the seed of an article about Robertson, but it wasn't the touchy-feely Christmas story her boss was looking for.

Ryan crossed his arms. "Anything you'd like to tell me?"

Heat spread across her cheeks but she shook her head. "I can't think of anything. Why?"

His sigh was half groan. "Tori, it's simple. I'm the Editor. You're the reporter. As such, when I give you an assignment, I expect you to do it. And I don't expect to get a phone call from the subject of said assignment explaining just how horrifically unprofessional my reporter has been."

"Unprofessional?" Tori shot to her feet and leaned toward Ryan. "I was the height of professional. He's the one who started off antagonistic with his dripping sarcasm about how the lights look better at night when they're lit. I mean really, duh. And then he refuses to answer even the simplest questions. Not exactly the behavior of a publicity hound looking for a feature about all his good deeds."

"Since that doesn't describe Gabe Robertson in any way, I'm not surprised. He mentioned the questions you asked. Frankly, Tori? I'm this close to giving you notice."

Her heart thundered in her chest. Fired? He'd fire her over this? How was that even possible? She'd done her job and gone to try and do the stupid popcorn piece. It wasn't her fault Gabe was still handsome, self-absorbed, and incapable of handling even the hint of criticism. She forced her voice to be calm. "On what grounds?"

"First, I don't need grounds in this state. But second? I sent you to do a feature promoting and highlighting his display. Asking him how much money he was stealing from people who thought they were making a charitable donation isn't the way to write that feature. And you know it."

"I didn't ask that." Not in so many words, at least. Even so, it was a valid question. In college, Gabe had been determined to make something of himself. And he'd absolutely defined success in terms of money in the bank. Given that, it wasn't unreasonable to assume he wasn't running an expensive light display on his own dime. No one changed their stripes that drastically.

Ryan held out his hand. "Give me your recorder."

Tori pulled her lower lip between her teeth. "I have notes for other stories on there."

"You don't have any other assignments right now. Hand it over."

She studied her boss' face. He wasn't going to be talked out of it. Her stomach twisted. She hadn't done anything wrong, but...she hadn't been as tactful as she could have been. Swallowing the bile that crept up her throat, she opened her desk drawer and pulled out the recorder, slapping it into his hand. "Fine. But I still contend I didn't do anything wrong."

"Noted." Ryan's hand curled into a fist around the recorder. "If this is as bad as Gabe said it was, you and I are going to have a problem."

Tori sank back into her chair as Ryan stalked off. Great. Now what? She clicked her word processing program back to full size and re-read the start to her article about Gabe Robertson. She'd drawn on her memories of him from college—and how had he not recognized her even a little? Had she truly been that forgettable? She drummed her fingers on her desk. Who was she still in touch with that she could get to give her more background on him?

4

"She said what?" Jake paced the length of Gabe's living room, his head shaking. "I hope you set her straight."

"I told her 'zero' and then asked her to leave."

"That's it? Man...you should've..."

"That was the old me, Jake. And the old you." Gabe dipped his hands into the pockets of his jeans. "I did call Ryan and let him know."

Jake gave a shark-like grin. "That's good. What'd he say?"

"That he'd look into it. That's enough." It would have to be. His temper was part of the old self he'd put off—and, it seemed, had to keep putting off—when Jesus had washed him clean. Gabe turned to look out the front window. A car turned into the driveway and parked next to Jake's truck. "I wanted the feature—still want it—to highlight OM. They're a good organization and what they do for the troops is more than just Christmas presents for lonely soldiers, since they focus on sharing the hope of our Savior's birth. You and I both know how important that is when you're stuck over there, facing what they do every day."

"But that was what, Saturday? It's Tuesday, and you haven't heard anything yet. You could try the *Post* and the *Times* again."

The doorbell rang, followed by a brisk knock at the door, saving Gabe from explaining for the hundredth time why he wasn't going back with his hat in his hand to the big papers. Not after the hatchet job they'd done on their intelligence company when they first started up. Were they military contractors? Sure. But they were solely support operations. Getting lumped in with people who were no better than mercenaries...Gabe clamped down on the thought as his blood began to boil. He jerked open the door with a bit too much force.

"Whoa. Am I late?" The gangly teen took a step back, glancing over his shoulder at his car.

Gabe lifted a hand in greeting to the boy's mom who sat in the car. She raised her book in her typical acknowledgement. He shook his head and smiled at Jared. "No, you're right on time. Maybe even early. None of the other guys are here yet. Come on in and grab a snack."

Gabe and Jake chatted with Jared about his high school basketball team as the other boys who attended the weekly Bible study slowly trickled in. Snacks were consumed before and during the lesson. When they'd closed in prayer, the boys huddled around the table, whispering.

"Something going on?" Gabe strolled to the snack area and snagged the last cookie.

The guys on either side of Jared nudged him in the ribs. Jared cleared his throat. "Any chance you'd turn on the lights and let us wander through?"

Gabe's eyebrows shot up. Not at all what he'd been expecting. Not that he'd had a clear idea what they'd ask, but more often than not when the guys huddled up like that, he'd ended up having to explain to parents why he hadn't warned them that he'd be answering questions about puberty or God's plan for sex.

The boys started chanting, "Lights. Lights. Lights."

With a laugh, Gabe held up his hands. The chanting stopped. "I'll turn on the lights on one condition."

The boys groaned.

Jake punched him on the shoulder. "Come on, man. Isn't this the whole reason you set up the display? What's with putting conditions on it?"

Gabe's grin stretched wider. "It's not that bad. Don't you even want to hear what it is?"

Gradually, the boys stopped groaning and nodded.

"At every section, we're going to stop and read part of Luke 2, and talk about how the cultural themes we see over and over at Christmastime ultimately feed back into the real reason for our celebration."

There were grumbles, as expected, but after a few minutes' debate, and with Jake's subtle encouragement, they all grabbed their coats and either a Bible or their cell with their Bible app open.

"That's the spirit. Come on. We'll start with an easy one— St. Nicholas." Gabe opened the front door and waited for the boys to file out before he hit the master switch for the light display. He jogged down the steps to the front of the cluster of kids and waved for them to follow him into the twinkling winter wonderland.

GABE SET his Bible aside and propped his feet up on one of his kitchen chairs, turning so he could gaze out the window. Thick frost coated the ground and the light displays, the ice crystals glinting in the slender fingers of sunlight that stretched down from the early morning sky. The words that the prophet Jeremiah wrote in Lamentations, part of his morning's reading, flickered through his mind. *The steadfast love of the Lord never*

ceases; His mercies never come to an end; they are new every morn-
ing; great is your faithfulness. His own life was a shining example
of that promise. Anyone who'd known him for more than the
last five years had seen the change from a hard-partying, self-
absorbed, ambitious...jerk—there really was no other word he
was willing to entertain—to the man he was today. And yet he
still fell short. Would he ever be able to redeem his past?

His cell buzzed with an incoming call. He frowned and
checked the ID. Huh. "Hey, Ryan. I didn't realize editors got
such an early start."

"Yeah, well. Old habits. I see you're not sleeping in."

"You don't know that."

Ryan snickered. "Yeah, I really do. Bet you've already had
three cups of coffee and spent time reading your Bible, too."

Gabe shook his head. Ryan had been instrumental in
showing him that relying on Christ didn't make him less of a
man. The habit of Bible study first thing was one he'd stressed
and Gabe clung to it. "Got me. What's up?"

The clatter of a keyboard rattled over the line for a moment
before Ryan spoke. "I think I've explained to Victoria that she
needs to do the article the right way now. I won't lie and say
she's on board, but she'll be there tonight with a photographer
to see the lights and do an in-depth interview. It means we
won't run the feature 'til Monday, but that still gets you a few
weeks of solid publicity."

He frowned and stared out the window. "If she doesn't want
to do it, why not assign someone else?"

"She's the best, Gabe. Real star potential and, between you
and me, the paper's lucky to have her. She has her sights set on
the big leagues. Would probably already be there if she could
keep a tighter rein on her..."

"Personality?"

Ryan let out a short laugh. "Sure. We can go with that. Look, she said something about hating Christmas, so there's clearly stuff going on in her personal life. Give her some grace?"

Gabe closed his eyes. Everyone needed grace. Who was he to deny it to anyone? "All right. You know I'm a big believer in second chances."

"I was hoping you'd say that. Look...is there any possibility you know her from somewhere?"

Know her? Gabe called up a memory of the stunning red-haired reporter from Saturday. Nothing jumped out at him or triggered a memory...and her face had been in his thoughts enough that he would've figured it out. "I don't think so. Why?"

"Mmm. It may be nothing, but she started a document on her machine here with a lot of background information about you. Looks like college-era stories, though nothing really bad. Honestly, it's almost like you were at least minimally friends, or you'd dated?"

Gabe swallowed, his stomach sinking. How much did she know about his past? "How...?"

"We don't actually have hard drives on these machines. They're more like terminals, so the articles are all stored on the server. Makes it easier to ensure that we don't end up editing the wrong version of something, nothing gets lost, that sort of thing. The reporters often forget that's the setup though. She was acting weird when I went to talk to her about how badly she botched last week, so I took a peek."

"Okay. Good to know. I guess." Should he know her? College was a blur. Some of that was simply the passage of time. The rest was the remnants of the not-quite-sober lifestyle that had carried him through those four years. "So, tonight? Any sort of ETA?"

It'd be good for him to be working the gate when she showed up. He could try and start the tour off on the right foot. If that was even possible. Worth a shot, at least.

"Not that I know of. But if she gives me something, I'll text you. And Gabe?"

"Yeah?"

"I haven't really explained our friendship. I'd rather not, if you can avoid it. It's not that there's anything wrong with doing a favor for a friend, but...it's easier if your display stands on its own merit. Which it does."

"All right. I appreciate it though."

"I owe you."

Gabe shook his head. Nothing was farther from the truth. "I'm not going to get into that argument with you again. Get to work."

He ended the call and blew out a breath. Interview with a prickly reporter, take two. At least she was pleasant to look at...until she opened her mouth and the abrasive started showing.

5

Tori tugged on the green sweater her dad had sent her when he took his new family on a vacation to Ireland. Another trip she would've enjoyed, if she'd been given the chance. She rubbed her hand over the intricate cable knitting. At least he'd remembered a souvenir. Her mother never even bothered with that. And she was stalling.

"Woodsie? Bernie?" Where had the cats gotten off to? She peeked in the closet, but they weren't curled around her shoes like they often were, despite her best efforts to keep them out of the closet. Should she wear something other than her low-heeled ankle boots? Maybe the tall boots? They looked good with skinny jeans...but the heel. If she was going to be tromping through a Christmas light display with paths of gravel or grass, she was better off with her first choice. "What's wrong with me? It's an interview. I do them all the time."

Woodward poked his head out from under the bed with an inquiring meow.

"There you are. Is Bernie down there too?" Tori knelt and scratched Woodsie's head as she looked around the flat storage boxes that held off-season clothes and keepsakes from high school and college. Bernie was tucked between two of them, his eyes gleaming in the darkness. "All right. Well, you boys be good, okay? I'll be back before you know it."

She stood and pressed a hand to her stomach. Interview. Not date. Not that Gabe would even be interested. The few times they'd had coffee were so she could help him cram for a test. She'd tried flirting, but her best efforts had zipped right over his head. Why would that have changed? He hadn't actually seemed to recognize her. That was fine. Better than fine. It was perfect.

Oh, who was she kidding? She'd wanted her chance to redeem a bad boy and had never even gotten off the starting block. Why was she still clinging to some fragile hope that she'd made any kind of impression on him beyond being a goody-two-shoes clinging to the fringes of the cool crowd? She'd been desperate then. She wasn't now.

The drive out to Clifton was as pleasant as trying to get anywhere on a Friday night in the D.C. Metro area could be. At least she was headed away from town. She frowned as she turned down the quaint main street. Who knew it was so busy on Friday nights? Twinkling white lights wound around trees and outlined the houses and stores. Families and couples strolled along the sidewalks, their breath visible in the crisp air. It was like a Norman Rockwell painting set in motion. Tori shook her head and followed signs to a public parking lot. She'd gotten away with parking in Gabe's driveway last weekend, but at night, with the light show underway? The event details the paper had run were very specific: no cars allowed on the property.

After locking her car, she slung her messenger-style purse over her shoulder and started toward Gabe's. A trickle of people, turning to a heavy stream, joined her until she found herself waiting in line to gain entrance. Soft Christmas music played from speakers hidden in the landscaping, setting a cheerful tone and making the wait bearable. It was almost enough to get her into the Christmas spirit. Almost.

She shuffled forward, finally reaching the small shed at the top of the driveway, decorated to look like a toll booth to the North Pole.

"Hi. Welcome to...Ah...Victoria, right?" Gabe's smile dimmed as he held out his hand. "Thanks for coming back when we're open."

She pasted on a bright, professional smile and gave his hand a brisk shake, ignoring the tingles that worked up her arm. "Thanks for having me."

"Hang on just a sec. I'll get Jake to come man the entrance and I can take you on a tour, answer whatever questions you have." He reached inside the booth and grabbed a bright yellow walkie talkie. His conversation was quick and quiet. "If you want to just step aside while we wait?"

Tori blinked, pulling her thoughts away from his lips. "Oh. Of course."

Gabe squatted down level with the kids in the family group that had been waiting behind her. "Hey there. You ready for a fun time?"

The kids grinned, nodding.

"Excellent." He stood and offered the parents a sheet of paper from the top of a stack. "Here's a map. It details the different neighborhoods and what you can expect at each one. We have three different choirs performing near the concessions and live Nativity tonight, so I hope you'll take a minute or two to relax and enjoy. And while admission is free, we're accepting donations for Operation Mistletoe here and at concessions. The back of the map tells you a little more about their mission."

"Thanks so much." The father of the kids stuffed a bill—was it a twenty?—into the donation bucket. "We started coming the first year you set up. It just keeps getting better."

"That's good to hear. Enjoy yourselves."

Tori watched as they consulted the map, the kids jumping up and down as they pointed to various spots on the paper. What must it be like to have that kind of enthusiasm for this time of year? And how was it possible for someone like Gabe to come across so personable, like he actually cared about anything beyond the money?

A man jogged up and slapped Gabe on the back. "Sorry it took me a minute, Doris needed the coffee pot moved and it was full. Too heavy for her and Dan to shift."

Concern flickered across Gabe's features. "You get them set?"

"Yeah, man. They're rocking back there. Go give your tour." The man flashed a sharp, toothy smile at Tori. "I've got this."

Gabe nodded and gestured for Tori to precede him. "If you don't have a preference, I thought we could follow what I consider the most meaningful path through everything. That work?"

Meaningful path? Through a bunch of lights in his yard? Granted, a large yard, and whole lot of lights. But meaningful? She shrugged. "Sure, why not? You mind if I record?"

"Sure, why not?" His words mimicked hers.

Was he making fun of her? She frowned and slipped her mini digital recorder out of her purse, clipping it on the strap near her shoulder. "So...why Christmas lights?"

"Seriously?" Gabe stopped and turned, tucking his hands in his pockets. He pursed his lips as his eyes held hers. "It's my second favorite time of year. But it's certainly the one most commonly considered happy."

"Second favorite? What's the first?"

He grinned. "Easter. Though that has some considerably mixed feelings that go with it."

"What's not happy about bunnies and candy? Honestly, I don't see a ton of difference between a fat man sneaking into houses to leave gifts and a rabbit hopping around hiding eggs. They're both ridiculous."

"Well, sure. If that's how you think about it. I take it you're not a believer?"

A believer. How long had it been since she'd thought of herself in those terms? College? Grad school? "I go to church, when I have the time, and believe in God, if that's what you're after. And okay, sure, Christmas is when Jesus came to Earth and Easter is His resurrection, but it's not as if either of those things help with day-to-day living."

Gabe's eyes clouded. "I'm sorry you feel that way. Helping people see that it's the exact opposite—that having Jesus in your life on a daily basis makes everything about life better—is one of the primary goals of this display. And of Operation Mistletoe. That's why the money we get, *all* of the proceeds, go to them."

She didn't miss his narrowed eyes as he emphasized the word 'all.' Tori fought the urge to scoff. Maybe she just had to figure out how he defined 'proceeds.' Didn't that usually mean after expenses were covered? With what it must cost to run all these lights, let alone the snacks and choirs, it didn't seem likely that the charity got very much. If anything.

She cleared her throat. "And have you always felt this way?"

"No. I'm relatively new to faith. After college, some friends and I started a company and landed a military contract to assist in intelligence operations overseas. Since we were so small, it was the three of us doing everything, and it meant we had to be right there, in the mix." Gabe paused, and stared out over the gleaming field of lights. "I don't know how anyone can be over there, see what's going on, and not question God. Thankfully, He put people in my path to help me turn toward Him, rather than away. And it's those experiences that feed the need to give back in whatever ways I can. This is just one of them."

He sounded sincere. It was just so hard to reconcile with her memories of him at college. He'd been so driven by money and success. Though it wasn't as if she was the exact same person she'd been then, either. Back then, she'd still expected God to hear her prayers and care one way or the other. "Mm. So tell me about this area...that's a lot of Santa lights."

THE CATS WOKE her at seven on Saturday. Just like they did every morning. They never seemed to care that she'd had a restless night. Her mom was always saying she should get one of those automated feeding bowls so they'd leave her be, but...it was nice to be needed. When she'd dished out their kibble and filled her extra-large mug with steaming black coffee, she sat at the tiny kitchen table and opened her laptop.

Where should she start with the article? Ryan's warning about playing nice rang in her ears, clashing with the image of drunk, college-aged Gabe with his arms around two sorority sisters and a third on his lap. She pushed away the twinge in her heart. Who had reformed him? That was supposed to have been her job or, at least, that's what she'd thought at the time. Maybe the change was just for show? It didn't matter. Couldn't. She needed to prove that she could hold the same job for a few years. Without that, her resume labeled her a risky hire, and that meant she wouldn't make it to the interview stage at any of the big papers.

Tori huffed out a breath and drew a knee up to her chest. She could do this. Old longings and still-humiliating rebuffs didn't have to play into it. Gabe had given her plenty of generic information about the light display and his desire to raise money for Operation Mistletoe that she could put something together. Would it please Ryan? There was no way to know until she handed it in. She opened a new document and began to type.

She'd barely gotten two sentences crafted when her cell rang. Biting back a groan, she answered. "Hello?"

"Victoria Spencer?"

"Yes?" Tori pulled the phone away from her ear and glanced at the Caller ID. Great. Probably selling something.

"Hi. This is Geneva Stearns, from the *Post*. We've been following your work at the *Tribune* for a while now and have a potential freelance opportunity."

At the *Post*? That could be huge. Her heart raced. "Oh. Gosh. Okay?"

"We're interested in doing a follow-up on an article from several years ago. It dealt, primarily, with small businesses looking to profit from the current tensions in the Middle East. Several of those companies are now defunct, however the one we're most interested in is still doing quite well."

"It sounds interesting. But...I have to ask, why call me?"

"It's...complicated. Still, I assure you, if you write the kind of expose I'm convinced you're able to produce, there could very well be a staff job opening up here with your name on it."

Her heart leapt into her throat. This could, finally, be her big break. "That sounds...amazing."

"I hoped you'd say that. If you'll give me a personal email address, I'll send you details and what background information we have. That should get you started. We'd need the final article before Christmas. Can you work in that timeframe?"

"That's not a problem." All she had going at the *Tribune* right now was the Christmas lights. She could even take some time off. Ryan wouldn't blink at that. She rattled off her personal email.

"I'll look forward to seeing your piece."

Tori's email chimed as she hung up the phone. Bouncing in her seat, she opened the message then clicked on the attached file. Gabe's face filled her screen, right next to the headline: INTELLIGENCE CONTRACTORS: WHOSE SIDE ARE THEY ON?

6

"How'd the interview go last night?" Jake hoisted himself onto the top of a picnic table, resting his feet on the bench.

Gabe snagged another piece of trash before it could blow away and stuffed it into the garbage bag he was holding. "Fine, I guess. I don't really get the idea that she's all that interested in the lights. Or the spiritual purpose behind them."

"Does she need to be? I mean really, all she has to do is write an article. Surely as a reporter she's used to writing about things that aren't all that interesting?"

"I guess." Gabe plopped onto the picnic table's bench. "It just seems like we'd get a better story out of someone who really got it. You know?"

Jake shrugged.

Gabe frowned. His friend had always had a more philosophical outlook on those kinds of things. It was one of the reasons he was a good asset to the company. Jake balanced out Rick and him. "Can you help again tonight? Last night's crowd was about twice what I'd expected given the lack of real advertising so far this year. Maybe word of mouth will do for me what this article isn't going to do."

"Sure. Can I hang back here with Doris? She gives me cookies."

Gabe laughed. Of course she did. "Yeah, that's fine. In the meantime, I dug through my college yearbooks last night. Spencer was in our class."

Jake blinked. "Really? Where'd she pledge?"

"She wasn't Greek. But seeing her photo, I realized she'd been in a few classes with me. Sociology, I think. Maybe Art History, too."

Jake drummed his fingers on his knee. "Red head...dude. Was she the girl who helped you with your final art project? The self-portrait in whatever classical style you wanted?"

Was that her? She'd had short hair and a broken leg from a skiing accident over the Christmas break for the first part of art class. Had her name been Victoria? "It might be. But I thought her name was Toni or Terri or something like that. Not Victoria."

"Tori, maybe?"

Gabe let out a short laugh. "Huh. Maybe. Wow. Small world. But it's not like we were friends or hung out."

"I'm not even sure why you went looking."

"Ah...I didn't mention Ryan's conversation, did I?" Gabe filled Jake in with a shrug. "Got me curious enough that I thought I'd poke around, see what I could find out."

"I don't suppose it hurt that she's pretty?"

Gabe fought a smile. That, right there, was Jake to a T. "Yeah, there's that, too."

Jake shook his head. "It's been nearly what, two years, since you took someone out? You finally get back in the game and it's with a reporter?"

"Who said anything about being back in the game? She's pretty and I apparently know her from college but...I've also been on the wrong end of her tongue. Acerbic is almost an understatement."

"Yeah, but you love a challenge."

Probably true. "Am I an idiot?"

Jake laughed. "That's a loaded question. Look around you, man. You use your yard as a Christmas light display just to spread cheer and, hopefully, plant one little seed that this time of year is about more than getting gifts."

"Funny guy. I'm serious."

Jake pursed his lips. "Nah. If you're interested, you ought to at least see if she is, too. No way to win if you never get in the game."

Gabe stood. Now he just had to figure out how to get a hold of her without it being weird. "I'm going to go check for trash through the rest of the display. If you want to be useful, you could start on the popcorn."

"You're even busier tonight."

Gabe looked up, right into Victoria's stunning blue eyes. His heart thundered in his chest and he fought to keep his tone casual. "Saturday night. People want to be out doing something, this is a nice stop along the way. What brings you back?"

"I forgot to take photos last night. My editor wasn't very happy with me. So..." Tori gestured to the camera slung around her neck. "Do you mind?"

"Not at all. Do you want some help? I can call Jake up to the front again."

She studied him for several heartbeats. "It's not an imposition?"

As if. This saved him from having to figure out a reason to call her. But she didn't need to know that. Yet. He grinned. "Not at all. And it keeps him from eating too many of Doris' cookies.

She's a soft touch when it comes to him. Says he reminds her of her son. Come on in the shack, out of the wind, and I'll give him a holler."

The space seemed even smaller with her in it. Why hadn't he noticed her perfume last night? It sent tingles through his chest every time he breathed in the earthy scent. He cleared his throat and called Jake to the front. "He's on his way. I should keep passing out maps 'til he gets here."

"I really can manage on my own. I don't mean to be a bother."

"You're not. It isn't." Gabe gave himself a hard mental kick. Could he sound any more like a mental patient? Sheesh. "I promised your editor that I'd help you with the article, so I want to make sure I do that."

Her eyebrows lifted, but she said nothing.

Gabe kept one eye on her as he repeated his welcoming spiel to the families that streamed through the entrance. She looked different tonight. Prettier, if that was possible. Her hair was down, falling in soft waves to her shoulders where a few strands were caught in the bright green scarf wrapped around her neck. The no-nonsense professionalism had softened into casual and warm. Which was the real Victoria?

"I thought I got to hang with Doris tonight." Jake reached around Gabe into the shelter for a stack of maps. "Oohhh. Got it."

Gabe shot his friend a look. "Victoria forgot to get photos last night. I thought I'd help."

"Good to see you again." Jake gave a brief nod then nudged Gabe in the side with his elbow. "I've got this. Go snap some pictures."

"Wait. Before we head off, why don't I get a picture of the two of you here at the entrance?" Tori took the lens cap off the camera and gestured for Gabe and Jake to stand next to one another. "That's great. Okay, say 'mistletoe.'"

The flash left spots dancing in front of his eyes. At least they replaced ethereal glow he'd been picturing floating around Victoria's head. The one that seemed to make her every movement slow down. "Did you have anywhere in particular you wanted to start?"

"Have fun you two." Jake's sing-song cut across the quietly playing Christmas music.

Gabe fought the urge to stick out his tongue.

"He really thinks he's a riot, doesn't he?" Tori shook her head and snapped the lens cap back on her camera.

"Yeah, but he's pretty harmless." Gabe took a breath. Maybe it was better to put all his cards on the table. "I think it's probably because I was telling him earlier that I knew you, sort of, in college. You probably don't remember..."

She turned, her gaze piercing his. "Oh, I remember."

He blinked. Was that a good thing or a bad thing? Her face was an unreadable mask. As shameful as it was, he didn't remember everyone he'd hooked up with in college but surely he wouldn't have forgotten her. Heat wormed its way up his neck. "Do I need to apologize to you? I know I wasn't the man I should have been in college. I only remember working on an art project together but..."

"Stop. We did the art project and had some good conversations over coffee and ice cream. You don't have anything to apologize for."

He raised his eyebrows and held her gaze for several seconds before nodding. "All right. Will you let me apologize, just generally, for being that kind of guy? And for not recognizing you faster? Someone as beautiful as you are should never have faded from my memory."

Her lips twisted into a wry smile. "Well, to be fair, you had a lot of female faces to keep straight."

Gabe winced. "Again, I'm sorry. I hope you'll give me a chance to show you that I've changed. I'm a living, breathing testament to the redemption available in Jesus for those who ask."

"This certainly seems to suggest that." She gestured to the light display. "You should call me Tori again. I really only use Victoria for my by-line. Now, how about we start with some photos of that leg lamp? That's not a setup you see everywhere."

Gabe chuckled and slipped his arm around her, putting his hand in the small of her back. Electricity sizzled up his arm. "We can get there faster this way. I didn't remember you wanted to go into journalism. Weren't you pre-med?"

"I was. Then I started looking at the reality of getting into medical school, let alone graduating." She shook her head. "It was more practical to find something that I could make a living at right away. I've always liked writing, so it was a good enough fit."

Good enough? That didn't imply a burning passion for her job. "And do you like it?"

"Sure. The *Trib's* a good place and, once I get some more credits to my name, I can jump to something with a bigger audience. Write stories that actually make a difference to people. You know, things that matter."

"As opposed to Christmas light displays."

Her hand flew to her mouth. "I didn't mean—"

"It's okay. People either understand why I do this or they don't. I'm grateful you're willing to write the story despite personal feelings. Here we are, one of my favorite secular Christmas movies." Gabe tucked his hands in his pockets. Was it worth trying to explain to her why it mattered? If there was any possibility of something between them, it would be worth it. But if her sights were set on big papers and hard-hitting stories maybe there wasn't enough common ground between them to bother.

Tori snapped a few pictures. "I'll admit, this is one movie I simply don't understand. Who cares if the kid gets a BB gun or not?"

"He does." Gabe smiled. "But the movie isn't about the BB gun, really. It's about family and growing up and just finding a way to remember the good parts of even the worst situations."

"You get all that from this?" She gestured to a set of lights depicting three men dressed in Chinese silk, their mouths open as if in song, with a duck on a platter in front of them.

"I do. Maybe you should re-watch the movie sometime."

"Is that an offer?"

His smile spread into a grin at the hint of challenge in her eyes. "Could be. Depends on your answer. Come on, you need to get some pictures of the Nativity. And then have a doughnut. Doris is making them fresh tonight."

7

Tori laughed as Gabe finished retelling a story about his first year doing the Christmas light display. The college boy she'd known would never have gone back for a second year. Not if their art project had been any indication. When his first attempt turned out badly, it had taken all her powers of persuasion to get him to sit down and try again instead of just taking a bad grade.

"Coffee or hot chocolate?" Gabe nodded toward the snack shack.

"Hot chocolate. It's just nippy enough that it's starting to feel like Christmas. And that means cocoa."

"You got it. Whipped cream? Marshmallows?"

"Yes."

He chuckled and skirted the line of families waiting for their refreshments.

Tori glanced at the small seating area. An eight-person group sang hymns acapella beside the live Nativity. It was peaceful. And it definitely highlighted the baby—it couldn't possibly be a real child, could it?—in the manger with the animals. Even with the secular displays, there was no question that Gabe's focus was on the birth of his Savior. Still, how did she reconcile that with his past? Or with the information Geneva had sent her this morning? Granted, most of it was speculation from five years ago. But to have made an article in the *Post*...it had to have some basis in the truth. Didn't it?

She pulled a plastic chair away from a two-person table tucked toward the back of the seating area and sat. She searched the crowd waiting for drinks. Her heart gave a jolt when she found him, ducking through the side door, balancing a covered plate and two steaming mugs. It had to be purely physical attraction. No warm-blooded woman could look at him, practically a walking L.L. Bean catalog ad, and not be attracted. And yet...

"Here you are. Good thinking, grabbing a seat. They're switching over to a full choir soon, so I suspect the area will fill up more as parents and siblings of the choir members come to hear."

"Clever way to get more folks through your display." Tori blew across the top of her steaming drink.

"I don't ask families of the performers to donate. I don't really ask anyone to donate—but I don't even mention it to the families. It really bothers you, doesn't it?" He leaned back in his chair, stretched out his legs, and crossed his ankles.

She frowned. "I don't know what you mean."

"You think I'm using this to line my own pockets. You're not even willing to try and believe that I do this because Operation Mistletoe is an organization I believe in."

Her chest tightened. She wanted to deny his words but...they weren't far off. She licked her lips. "It's just hard to imagine, I guess. All this has got to cost a small fortune. And for what?"

His lips thinned. "First, I can afford it. Even without my share of my parent's estate I could afford it. Our company is doing well enough that we turn business down. We'd have to hire too many people too quickly to handle all the opportunities we're offered. And frankly, Jake, Rick, and I want our teams to be small, like family. That can't happen overnight. But even with that? None of us—and that includes every member of our team—is hurting for money. So if I wanted to run this year round, I could. The power company might get annoyed at how much I was using, but not because I couldn't pay my bills."

Tori blinked. Why would he tell her this now but not when she first asked? If only she had her recorder...maybe that was it. This was him, talking to a—what? Friend? Hardly. Woman he was interested in? She fought the urge to snort. Right. "I didn't mean to offend you."

"Second, even if I couldn't afford it? I'd hock everything I had to give back to Operation Mistletoe. They saved my life. Literally and figuratively. The first two years of the business, when it was just Jake, Rick, and me, were rough. Being over there...it's not anything I can explain. That first Christmas, I was on the verge of giving up on everything. The company, sure. But life, too." Gabe stared across the crowded dining area toward the Nativity.

Tori reached across the table and rested her finger tips on his arm, ignoring the heat of the contact. It was hard to imagine this man—the Gabe she'd known in college *or* the one sitting with her now—ever being at such a low point. "I'm sorry."

He turned and held her gaze. He gave a terse nod and his voice was still husky with emotion. "So you see, this isn't completely altruistic. I have to give back. I get a very real, very deep personal reward from doing this. Not monetary. Much, much more valuable than that."

∼

TORI TURNED off the engine and stared at the large building. What was she doing? She could go back home, spend her Sunday the way she usually did, curled up with all the major U.S. newspapers and her cats. But...something about the way Gabe had issued the invitation last night after he'd walked her back to her car had her agreeing before her brain caught up. Now she was here. It wasn't as if she'd given her word...but she might as well have. She wasn't someone who agreed to something and then flaked out.

She bit her lip, the excited response to Geneva she'd dashed off without a thought leaping to mind. Was this part of her research? Was that why she'd agreed? Her stomach lurched. The article had seemed like a golden opportunity. Before she spent the evening with Gabe with no voice recorder standing between them. Even in college, when it was clear they were from two different worlds, conversation had been easy. That hadn't changed.

Tori growled and grabbed her purse as she thrust open the car door. It was church. She'd grown up going. Mostly. Maybe Mom had slacked off some after Dad left, but they'd been there more often than not. She'd go in, find a seat in the back, and rush out as soon as it was over. Then she could honestly tell him she'd been there, if he asked. She would just have missed him. In a church this size, that was a definite possibility. Probability, even.

She pulled open the foyer door, the wall of heat and noise slamming into her. Whoa. She pushed in and slid along the edge of the crowd, her eyes scanning the signs that dangled from the ceiling. How were you supposed to know where the sanctuary was? She bounced off a solid wall of warm wool.

"Oh, I'm so sorry. I wasn't looking..." Tori trailed off as her gaze met Gabe's.

He offered an amused grin. "Told you I'd find you. I'm glad you made it."

She tried to be annoyed, but her heart was beating too fast

and every nerve ending was on fire with thrilling shocks. She cleared her throat. "So you did. How is that possible?"

He laughed and tucked her arm through his. "I took a guess that you'd park in the bigger lot. Most visitors do. From there, these are the most obvious doors. So I parked myself nearby and waited. Still, you've got the skulking around the fringe of a crowd thing down so well, I might have missed you if you hadn't slammed into me."

Skulking? She frowned. "I was just trying..."

"To avoid finding me. I get it. But now you're stuck. Come on. I like a woman who keeps her word even when she's not sure she wants to. Have you been here before?"

Tori bristled. How could he read her so accurately? No one else—not even her parents, or perhaps especially not her parents—was able to do that. "I don't think so. Church shopping hasn't been as high on my list as maybe it should've been."

"Well, you're in for a treat. Pastor Brown is the best." Gabe turned and led her through the crowd, offering a raised hand in greeting here and there as people called out his name.

"Slow down. Some of us aren't six feet tall."

He flashed a grin. "Six-two. Sorry. It's the crowds. I get itchy, right at the back of my skull. All I can think is 'get through and get out.'"

PTSD? Had to be. But he was in intelligence. Civilian intelligence, at that. Had they seen combat? That seemed unlikely, but his behavior, and some of the things he'd said last night, certainly suggested he had. "So why stay here? Why not find a smaller church? Something more comfortable?"

He shrugged. "Pastor Brown. Besides, I usually avoid the main lobby. I know all the back ways to get from here to there. And sometimes I make it a point to get here a few minutes late, once the crowds thin. It's not so bad. Here we go."

Tori slipped through the door he held open. The sanctuary was enormous, but it felt like a sanctuary, not a big auditorium as so often happened with the large spaces. The pews were already filling, but there was still plenty of room. Maybe not for everyone out in the lobby, but there had to be small groups going on right now too. "Do you have a usual spot?"

"I like the back row, but we can scoot closer if that's better for you."

She shook her head and slid into the pew, working her way to the middle. "This is fine."

Gabe sat beside her, just far enough away that their legs didn't touch. Though he was likely to bump her if either of them shifted much. She glanced at him out of the corner of her eye as she arranged her purse and Bible next to her. Was he really interested in her? Or was this just his way of ensuring she wrote a positive piece about his light show? And why did he want the publicity so badly? What was he hiding?

"You okay?" Gabe's breath tickled her ear.

She nodded and pushed aside that train of thought. Now wasn't the time. She'd do her research and see where the truth ended up.

THE SERVICE WAS BETTER than she'd expected. The music did a good job spanning the style preferences of the broad age range in the pews. But the best part was that every song was full of Christ. There wasn't one that could be mistaken for a love song to a boyfriend. That had been the beginning of the end to her church attendance her last year of college. She hadn't been able to figure out who she was supposed to be singing to, or about. And yet, everyone else raved about how uplifting their worship experience had been. Tori had figured she was doing some-thing wrong. And if she couldn't get something as simple as singing along, what possible chance was there to succeed at anything else when it came to Christian living? But, sitting here with Gabe, it felt like maybe there was hope after all.

As the organ started in and the people around them stood, gathering their things, and heading for the exits, Gabe turned to her, one eyebrow cocked. "Well?"

"You were right. Pastor Brown is special. He...it's like he actually gets what real life is like."

Gabe chuckled. "That's a good summary. I don't know the whole story, but I think he's had some rough knocks in the last several years. So even if he didn't get it before, he definitely does now. Hungry?"

On cue, her stomach growled. She didn't want to turn this into a date. Did she? "Yeah, but..."

"No pressure. Thanks for coming this morning."

Tori frowned. He was giving up? Just like that? "You're an irritating man, do you know that?"

A furrow appeared in his forehead. "Sorry?"

She sighed. "I'd like to go to lunch with you."

"But you said..."

"I know what I said, okay? It was knee-jerk. So...lunch? Please?"

One corner of his mouth quirked up. "Well, since you said please. How do you feel about barbecue?"

8

Tori perched on the edge of one of the comfortable leather chairs in the lobby of Intelligence Associates, Incorporated while she waited for the receptionist to finish her call. Other than the world clocks arranged in a row on the dividing wall between the lobby and main hall, the offices were typical Arlington contractor spaces, barely distinguishable from one to the next.

"Good morning. I'm sorry about that, can I help you?" The receptionist offered a polite smile.

Tori stood and crossed to the desk. "It's not a problem. I'm Victoria Spencer, from the *NoVa Tribune*. I'm doing an article on your CEO's Christmas display and was hoping to get a little more background on him and the company to help fill it out."

"Have you talked to Mr. Robertson?"

"I spoke with him over the weekend, when I was taking photos of the lights." Tori smiled. It wasn't completely a lie. She had spoken to him. She hadn't asked permission to come and poke around the office, but if the receptionist assumed he was okay with it, Tori wasn't going to say anything.

"I can give you a quick tour of the public areas. We do a lot of sensitive and classified work, you understand, so those areas are completely off limits, even to some of the staff." The receptionist punched some buttons on the phone and stood. "I'm Angel. Can I get you some coffee or tea?"

"No, thanks. Is it okay if I use a digital recorder?" Tori slipped the pen-like device from her purse and held it out.

Angel pulled her lip between her teeth before slowly nodding. "Okay. But no pictures."

"Sure thing. Thanks, I appreciate it. I've read up on the company from your website, so you can skip that. But I'd love to hear what you think about working here."

Angel beamed. "This way is the conference room and kitchen. I love it here. I've had a number of different reception jobs. This is the first one where the whole company is family. Even the front desk. I mean, the guys—not that the analysts are all men, but everyone just calls them 'the guys'—are definitely second families. They have to be with the hours they work when things get hot. But Mr. Robertson, Mr. McGill, and Mr. Wentworth go out of their way to make sure that no one gets left out."

Tori poked her head into the conference room when Angel gestured through the door. It didn't have any of the luxurious appointments she'd expected, but the basic functionality was there. They must pour their profits into something other than conference room furniture. "Oh? How do they do that?"

"Well," Angel stopped and cast a furtive look over her shoulder, "the biggest way is benefits. Everyone gets paid well above scale. Even me. But there's also the benevolence fund—that's what they call it. It's a fund that the owners set up and maintain from their personal finances and if anyone has a financial need that they can't meet, all they have to do is ask. They paid for my daughter's choir trip to London. She wasn't going to be able to go, just no way for us to scrape together our part of the money. But Mr. Robertson overheard me talking about it and the next thing I knew, he was handing me a personal check."

"Wow. That's...generous. I guess the choir named him in the program?"

"Oh, no. No. That's part of the deal. If you get money from the BF, you're not supposed to mention it." Angel's cheeks burned red. "Oh, please, you can't use that in your article. It's just so you understand. These men? They're *good* men. And they've built a good company. One that cares."

Tori nodded. Where was the angle? Who gave away money like that without getting some publicity from it? "So just little things like school trips?"

Angel hesitantly shook her head.

"Look, I promise I won't use it. But I'm trying to get a feel for the man behind the light display, you know? He hasn't exactly been the darling of the media in past years."

"Those articles." Angel frowned. "No research, just hearsay and speculation. I'm surprised the *Post* didn't fire that Stearns woman. Everyone thought Mr. Robertson should sue, but he wouldn't. Said if we ignored it, it'd go away. I guess he was right, but it would've felt better to see her on the street or writing ad copy for the bargain store catalogs."

Stearns had been the initial reporter? Why wasn't her by-line on any of the information she'd sent? And if the article hadn't gone anywhere, why was the *Post* doing a follow up so many years later? Tori tucked the questions away. She'd need to do more research tonight. "You see what I mean though."

Angel chewed her lip. "I do. I don't have details on much. Most people keep it to themselves, but you might mention something to a friend, you know? I had a good friend who did admin work for the three owners. She lost her husband in a car accident, has two little ones at home. The bosses cut her hours to 'as needed,' set her up so she could do most of it at home, and gave her a raise. She's able to be home with her babies now more than when he was alive. It's not as good as having her man, but what other company does more than give you a week off for bereavement leave?"

"That's...generous." Incredibly so. "Do you think she'd talk to me?"

"Probably not. I can send her your contact information though. Then if she wants to, she will." Angel led the way down a hall and back out to the reception area. "We have very little turnover here. Like I said before, it's a family more than an office. And I guess if you need more background information, you'll want to talk directly to Mr. Robertson."

Tori recognized a dismissal when she heard it. She smiled. She'd gotten more than the shoulder-to-shoulder stonewalling she'd expected, but the picture painted was very different than what she'd imagined. "Thank you for your time, Angel. I appreciate it."

TORI RUBBED her eyes and dropped her head back on the couch cushions. She'd been digging around online and chatting with various contacts for, she checked the clock, almost four hours. Nothing. Just the one series the *Post* did at the start of their company had anything bad to say about Gabe or Intelligence Associates, Inc. It honestly felt so clean that it was suspicious. But the private investigator she knew who owed her a favor hadn't been able to turn up anything more than a couple of speeding tickets given to Rick Wentworth. Gabe even got permits from the city council for his light display. They weren't required, technically, since he was on private property, but apparently he really wanted it completely above board.

"Now what, Woodsie?" She rubbed his head before uncurling from the couch and stretching. Her muscles screamed and her right foot tingled as the blood started moving and waking it up. The cat sent her a baleful glare before hopping off the couch and stalking into the kitchen. Tori chuckled. A snack wasn't a bad idea.

Bernie hunched by his bowl, shifting slightly as Woodsie jumped up next to him. Tori dropped a handful of treats into each bowl. She jumped when her cell began to jangle from the counter.

"Hello?"

"Vic—Tori? Hi. It's Gabe. Robertson?"

She laughed. He sounded like a nervous teenager. "Hi. How are you?"

"Good. I'm good. Um, I'm not interrupting something, am I? You're probably working, right?"

"I just took a break, actually. It's almost eight. Even reporters stop writing every now and then. What's up?"

"Ha. Good to know." Gabe's breath crackled in her ear. "I was wondering if you might want to have dinner some night this week. I can't do weekends right now, obviously, but I was hoping a weeknight might work."

Adorable. Or maybe it was just the echo of all the fabulous things Angel had said about him at the office. A combination of them? The harsh indictments of Geneva Stearns' article flitted through her mind. But she hadn't found any evidence, and she'd tugged on as many lines as she could think of. "I do eat on weeknights."

He chuckled. "I'm bungling this. Let me put my cards on the table. I like you and I'd like to go on a date or two. Or more. And see if there can be anything between us."

Tori sagged against the counter. Who did that? Who put it all out there so matter-of-factly? No one, that's who. She pressed her hand to her breastbone, but it did nothing to calm her pounding heart. It was sweet. And almost insulting. She couldn't quite keep the insult out of her voice. "I'm...not quite sure how to respond to that."

"How about, 'Yes, Gabe, I'd love to have dinner with you tomorrow night.'?"

Tori snickered. "Yes, Gabe, I'd love to have dinner with you on Thursday night."

"Thursday?"

"I've got a thing tomorrow. And Wednesday."

"Thursday it is. I'll pick you up at six?"

She drummed her fingers on the counter. "How about I meet you?"

He made a buzzing noise. "My mother, rest her soul, would kill me."

"All right. Six." She rattled off her address. "What should I wear?"

"Something like you did on Saturday would be great. See you then."

"Yeah. See you." Tori hit 'end' and set down the phone. What was she doing?

9

Gabe threw his shoulders back and stared at Tori's door. He'd been on dates before. He'd even dated after he became a Christian. Of course, those dates hadn't turned out quite the way he'd planned. Maybe he'd been naive, but he'd expected Christian women to be committed to abstinence before marriage. The fact that they all weren't had blindsided him. That was part of the man—boy—he was trying to leave behind. Ultimately, it had pushed him away from dating all together. But Tori...didn't strike him as the kind of woman who was just out for a good time. He'd find out, one way or the other.

He knocked on the door and tucked his hands in his pockets. Should he have brought flowers? He'd talked himself out of them, and back in and then back out again, more times than seemed reasonable. Ultimately, he'd decided to try and go with a friendly tone rather than romantic.

Tori opened the door and his mouth went dry. "Ah, wow. You look amazing."

She grinned. "I'm not quite ready yet. Come on in and give

me just another couple minutes. Woodward and Bernstein are around somewhere, they'll probably come say hi."

He frowned. "The journalists?"

"My cats. But I'm impressed you caught the reference." She laughed. "Have a seat."

From the edge of the sofa, he watched her pad down the hallway, the bare skin of her ankles drawing his attention back to the leggings that hugged shapely legs. The royal blue sweater was long enough to be a dress and perfectly modest, but it launched his senses into overdrive anyway. He should've brought flowers.

A giant cat jumped onto the couch and smacked his hand with its head. Gabe held still and let it sniff his fingers before gingerly scratching behind its ears. Another monster cat leapt up on the other side, demanding attention with vigorous yowls. Given their size, it was possible the beasts had eaten their namesakes. They seemed friendly enough, but cats...you had to be careful around cats.

When the cats settled in and were no longer watching him, he let his gaze roam around the living room while he continued scratching their ears. It wasn't quite what he'd expected. The lack of frilly, overtly girly decor wasn't the surprise. He'd pegged Tori as a straightforward woman and that tended to be reflected in cleaner lines and less fussy furniture. But this teetered—precariously—on the edge of sparse. Like she'd just moved in or wasn't planning to stay very long.

"The boys being nice?" Tori came back down the hall. She'd pulled her hair back into a loose knot at the nape of her neck and tall leather boots now encased her legs to the knee.

Gabe nodded. "They seem to like me. Though I didn't realize you could domesticate mountain lion cubs."

Tori snickered. "They're part Maine Coon and they're not *that* big. Do you not like cats?"

Was this a test that he was about to fail? He lifted a shoulder. "I don't dislike them. I guess I haven't been around enough of them to form a firm opinion either way."

"No pets growing up?"

"Not really. I used to try and take in strays—cats, dogs, rabbits that happened to hop through our yard. But my parents weren't having it. We moved a lot, anyway."

"Well, that explains it."

"What?"

Tori shook her head. "Every time I've been to your house or to the light display, I've been looking for your dog. Land like that, you should have at least one dog. But with the people coming and going with the lights, I couldn't figure out where you kept him so he didn't steal everyone's treats."

Gabe smiled. He kicked around the idea of a dog every now and then. But even though he was based here now, he still had to go overseas to check on things in the flesh now and then, or to give Jake and Rick a break. If he had a dog, he'd have to find a house sitter or board it or something...it sounded like a pain. Given how tenderly she was petting her cats, it was probably best not to phrase it that way. "Ready?"

"Sure." Disappointment flickered across her features before she smiled back.

Had he ruined his chances by not being gung ho about pets? Surely there were more important things to consider? He didn't have anything *against* them. Should he say that? Maybe it was better to just change the subject. "Did you enjoy the tour of the office on Monday?"

She turned from gathering her purse, her hand on the door knob, cheeks a bright red. "I did. You have a nice-looking operation. I was going to mention that tonight."

Was she? Why hadn't she mentioned it when they'd talked on Monday night? Hadn't he asked what she'd been up to? Maybe not. Still. It nagged at the back of his mind. What was she hoping to accomplish? Angel said she'd just taken a quick look, asked a few basic questions, and left. But there was something off. "I would've taken you around, if you'd asked."

"I thought you were on vacation for the month, doing your light display."

Gabe held open the passenger door of his car for her. She slid in and he closed it with a gentle *thunk*. Crossing the front of the car, he tried to push down his irritation. He climbed in behind the wheel.

"You're never really on vacation when you own the company. I still check in—even go in—a couple days a week. Jake's completely off, since he's based overseas right now. But since this is my usual office, I'm available when I'm needed."

Tori clasped her hands in her lap. "Sorry. I just wanted to get a feel for it, see if there was anything to add to the article. Ryan mentioned he wanted to highlight the man behind the lights. I figure with you, a lot of that is your company."

It made sense when she said it that way. He gave a curt nod. "No big deal. So how's the story coming?"

"I sent the copy to Ryan this morning. It'll run tomorrow. I know there's only one more full weekend before Christmas..."

Gabe shrugged. There was nothing he could do about it. "Any little bit helps. As it turns out, my accountant says we're already close to double what we gave last year. So maybe word of mouth is starting to kick in."

"That's great." Tori turned and looked out her window. "Where are we headed?"

"Ah, now. That's for me to know, and you to find out. But I hope you're hungry." Gabe grinned and shifted lanes. The Irish Pub in Arlington was a favorite for work lunches and though he hadn't been for dinner, the menu was the same. If they had live music, it'd be even better. But the best part was that they could park under his office building and then hop on the Metro for the second half of the evening's entertainment.

The rest of the drive was pleasant. Their conversation

shifted from one topic to another. Was it because she was a reporter that she had so many opinions on such a wide variety of issues or was she, like him, just naturally curious?

"Here we are."

Tori pursed her lips. "Your office building?"

"Just around the corner. But this is free parking." He led her out to the street and directed her along the sidewalk with a gentle hand on the small of her back.

She chuckled. "Clever. Is that why you rented space in Arlington instead of Tyson's Corner?"

"Nah. This is closer to the Pentagon. Since they're our biggest client, there's no point in being farther away than necessary. From here, it's an easy Metro ride to get to meetings. And some of the folks we coordinate with are around and easily accessible, too. Just made more sense. But the parking is a nice bonus." Gabe held open the heavy wood door of the Pub.

"Smells incredible in here."

"I always think so." Gabe held up two fingers to the hostess. She beckoned for them to follow as she wound between tables and into the less-crowded back room. "Thanks."

Tori flipped open the menu. "What's good?"

"I haven't had a bad choice yet, but I'm particularly fond of the fish and chips." Gabe rubbed his sweating palms on his jeans. Had choosing something so casual been a mistake? Would she have preferred linen table cloths and candlelight? That just wasn't him. He'd made the effort in the past, but then women expected it. And they didn't understand that sometimes there was nothing wrong with eating directly from a bag of chips—not a bowl—on the couch and catching a game. No point in encouraging false expectations.

"This is great." Tori snapped the menu shut. "I haven't had fish and chips in a long time. Not good ones, at least. I don't think I realized this place was here, and I've driven down the road fairly often. Crazy."

The tightness in his chest eased. "Hopefully you'll like what's next, too."

TORI TRIPPED on the edge of the escalator as it lifted them to street level. Gabe grabbed her arm. "You okay?"

"Yeah. Other than being mortified. Who trips on an escalator?"

He chuckled and slid his hand down her arm. Their fingers brushed, sending sparks up his arm. Should he? He curled his fingers around hers. "I imagine it's more common than you know."

Tori's gaze flicked down to their joined hands then back to his face. She smiled and looked around. "So...somewhere in D.C.?"

Gabe squinted up at the street sign and gave her hand a light tug. "Look this way."

The back of the White House glowed a few blocks away.

"It's so pretty. I love seeing it lit up at night, though I hardly ever do. I don't really like coming downtown."

"I don't mind if I don't have to drive." Gabe grinned. "Come on, it's just a little bit of a walk."

Tori didn't take her hand back. He considered that a good sign as they walked past the side of the White House, toward the very-crowded Ellipse.

"Where are we...the Christmas trees?"

"Absolutely. Where else can you see an enormous Christmas tree surrounded by fifty smaller ones, all decorated by school children? And they have reindeer. You know you want to feed a reindeer."

She shook her head. "I can say with absolute certainty that I have never, *ever*, wanted to touch a reindeer."

Gabe stopped and met her gaze. "No Santa growing up? The Night Before Christmas? None of it?"

"Oh, sure. Mom and Dad did the whole shebang. But it never made sense. I mean, flying reindeer? Who makes this stuff up? And even if you go so far as to be okay with the behemoth flying forest creatures, why does everyone have their very own herd of eight full-sized reindeer that we're supposed to believe are really Santa's? *Pfft.*"

"Shh." Gabe pulled her further down the path, away from the scowls of parents with small children. "We can skip the reindeer. Can we at least walk through the trees? Or...if you really don't want to, I can just take you home."

"No, it's okay. Let's see the trees. Maybe I'll work up some interest in deer feeding while we're at it. I just...Christmas and I have a long and horrific history. I know you're into the whole 'most wonderful time of the year' bit, and hey, that's great. But for me it's usually just a disaster." Tori pulled her hand away and tucked them into her coat pockets.

Gabe frowned and followed suit. He could still feel the outline of her hand in his. "Maybe this year'll be different."

10

Tori stared at the clock. At this point, she might as well get out of bed and start the day. The cats, at least, would be on board with the early start. It was definitely going to be a day for coffee. But what else could she do? Ryan didn't have any new assignments for her—he was probably punishing her for the rocky start with the article about Gabe. Still...it was the week before Christmas. There weren't a lot of stories to get out right now, not for a tiny paper that focused on the local scene. National news? International? Sure, there was plenty going on. But she didn't cover those stories. Yet.

She shuffled to the kitchen and hit 'brew' on the coffee machine before scooping kibble into the boys' bowls. Tori watched them eat until the beep signaling the end of the brew cycle startled her out of her reverie. She filled a mug and carried it to the kitchen table where she'd left her laptop plugged in.

Tori slid her finger across the touchpad to wake the machine and logged into her email. Another message from Geneva greeted her. Her stomach twisted as she opened it.

Victoria-

Just checking in to see how your article is coming. I'm including the contact info for the man I spoke to when we did the initial investigation. He's happy to talk to you, too.

Looking forward to seeing a draft whenever you get it.

-G

Tori blew out a breath. This article could be the start of something big. The *Post*, for crying out loud. But...why hadn't someone at Gabe's office given even the slightest indication that there was more going on behind the doors than appeared? And the fund for employees? That wasn't something even major Fortune 500-type companies did. You had to have an honest, caring heart to use your own money for something like that. On the other hand...that first article painted Gabe and his partners as vultures, looking to profit from the spoils of war. Major newspapers fact-checked articles before they ran them, didn't they? So...it had to be true. Even if that idea simply didn't sit right.

She closed the email without responding.

Okay, God. Here's the thing. I know we haven't been on the best of terms lately. My fault. Obviously. But I don't know what to do. You've got to get tired of people ignoring You and then running back when they need help—sorry. I was going to turn things around first, it was on my list...well, You know that. Of course, I never got to it. But...Gabe's special somehow. And I don't want to be the kind of reporter who does whatever it takes to see her by-line picked up by the AP. Integrity. I want to have it. Please...please help me know what to do.

THE FOOD COURT at the Ballston mall was packed. Of course, it was noon on a Friday in the heart of Arlington. Everyone was probably on their lunch break and, for whatever reason, they'd chosen the mall over the nicer places to eat. Or maybe it was always this busy. Tori scanned the area for an empty table. There was a group of four who looked like they were starting to clear their trash. She scooted between chairs and hovered near the group as they collected their things and slid into one of the chairs as soon as they'd picked up the last tray.

"Crowded today."

Tori grinned at the young woman. "A lot like the parking lot. Guess everyone's finishing up their shopping."

"Don't remind me. I have to come back here after work." The woman waved and disappeared into the crowd.

Why had this guy suggested a mall? At Christmas. Wouldn't it be safer to meet up somewhere private, where it was less likely they'd be seen than here in the middle of half the population of Arlington? And how was she supposed to recognize him? Tori groaned. This was doomed.

"Pardon me, is someone sitting here?"

She looked up and met the gaze of a man who looked to be in his late twenties. "I'm expecting someone."

"Ms. Spencer?"

"Yes?"

The man offered a tight smile as he pulled out a chair. "I'm Hewitt."

Not at all what she'd expected. Younger, to start. With hard lines around his mouth and eyes. He clearly didn't smile much. "Thank you for agreeing to meet me."

"Anything to help the world see the true Gabe Robertson. Though I'm not sure what I can tell you that's different from what I told Geneva five years ago. I quit shortly before the article was published." Hewitt folded his hands on the table in front of him.

She wanted to get out her recorder, but given the set of his mouth, that wouldn't go over well. "Maybe you could start with how you know Mr. Robertson and Intelligence Associates."

His lips thinned. "There were originally four founders to IA, Inc. The plan, at the outset, was to develop a software product that assisted intelligence agencies in doing their job. It was never the plan for us to be involved beyond technical support for that software product. We started out that way, but development costs were running high, implementation hit some snags, and the three of them decided to go after in-country contracts to help defray expenses. They left me here to oversee product development."

"So what happened?" None of that sounded significant. It wasn't as if they shut him down and dragged him with them.

"What happened is they went off to the Middle East and I got stuck with incompetent programmers who, one by one, all quit. There was no way I was going to be able to write the software myself and I couldn't hire people fast enough, and get them up to speed. Production stalled, before stopping all together. And when I asked Gabe, Jake and Rick what I should do, they said let's put it on hold. Get on a plane and head over here, we could use the help." He made a dismissive face. "As if I was going to do that. It's like they forgot who I was."

Tori raised her eyebrows. Was she supposed to know who he was, too? She'd have to look it up. Maybe Geneva had included his last name somewhere in her notes. "That must have been frustrating."

"That's an understatement. So then they told me that if I wasn't going to support the current thrust of the business, that they couldn't justify my salary. They bought back my shares and I was out. Just as well, because then Geneva's article was published and they took a hit for about a year, scraping along hand to mouth without my money. Frankly, I'm surprised to hear they have enough business now that anyone's interested in doing another article on them."

"When you left, did they keep your intellectual property? Or cheat you in some way?"

"They let me keep the software specs, said they'd changed their minds and wanted to be a service provider rather than a product. But without their brains to feed the knowledgebase, the product is useless, even if I could find programmers competent enough to put it together."

"Is that what you're doing with your new company?" Tori couldn't understand why Hewitt was so upset. From everything he said, they'd been fair, particularly given that he left voluntarily after they'd given him a chance to stay.

He shook his head. "Nope. I'm completely out of that game and back in banking. It's the family business. And at least I know no one's going to pull the rug out from under me and say we're suddenly shifting into paper mills or something else completely crazy."

A light bulb went off in Tori's head. Hewitt plus banking and the social pedigree of his family hit her. How had IA, Inc. survived after Hewitt pulled out his family money and, she had to assume, made it more difficult to get financing from other banks?

"So. You're going to do another column on them, finally make sure they're seen as what they are?"

"I'm still in the research phase at this point. I'm not even sure there's enough for an article. Like you said, they've kept a low profile. Hypothetically, what is it you're hoping will be revealed?"

Hewitt leaned across the table. "They're backstabbers. The plan was to do software. And just because you run into some problems, you don't ditch the whole idea and completely shift focus and leave the rest of your company hanging."

"I thought they were taking contracts to fund the software development? Isn't that what you said?"

"Sure, that's what they said. But I saw the truth. Leaving me here by myself with an incapable staff and an incomplete software design. What was I supposed to do? That software was all out of Rick's head. He'd put the plan together and done most of the staffing."

Tori's fingers itched for a notepad. "So why didn't he stay and you go overseas?"

"Oh, he offered. But you're missing the point."

Was she? It seemed that Hewitt had expected all the benefits of being one of the founders without having to do any of the work. And if it was this obvious five years later, how was it possible for Geneva to miss? "Okay. What's the point?"

"They set me up!" Hewitt slammed his fist on the table, drawing the attention of some of the nearby diners. He took a deep breath and pressed his palms flat on the table. "Once you've reached an agreement on something like this, you don't change it. Certainly not without the decision being unanimous. No, they got together behind my back and figured out the one way to get me to leave. And then they act all magnanimous, offering to buy back my investment at double what I put in."

"Double?"

He gave a jerky nod. "Just wanted to be sure I didn't feel cheated down the line, they said."

Tori squirmed. This was, hands down, the most pointless interview she'd ever done. He wasn't a confidential source. He was a spoiled brat looking for people to listen to him whine. "Mmm. I have another appointment and should run. Thanks for your time."

"That's it?" Hewitt scowled. "That's nothing different than the first article."

"Well...do you have something new to add?"

"Nothing concrete, mind you. But if I was you, I'd be looking into the company's financials. And the personal finances of the three owners. I'm sure they're skimming off the top or inflating rates. Something." Hewitt's face was flushed and he waved his arms in the air.

"Okay. I'll keep that in mind. Thanks again for your time." Tori stood and grabbed her purse. She strode down the hall, forcing herself not to look back lest he be encouraged and try to follow her. What a waste of time.

11

G abe punched Tori's number into his cell. He leaned against the kitchen counter as it rang and looked out the window at the backyard. Hopefully, with the article they ran yesterday, the crowd this weekend would be even better.

"Hello?"

"Hi Tori, it's Gabe. I wanted to say thanks for the article. You did a nice job." Gabe paused, listening to the noise in the background—a combination of talking people and Christmas Muzak. "Are you at the mall?"

"Ugh. Yes. I don't know what possessed me. All these people. And the Christmas stuff is everywhere. Why do people get so tangled up in this holiday?"

Gabe's lips twitched. "They're not, really. Not in the important part, at least."

Her sigh crackled the speaker of his phone. "Which just solidifies my feelings on the whole thing. It's become all about gimme, gimme, gimme and spend, spend, spend. And for what? A big family to-do that, ultimately, leaves you depressed for the next two weeks."

His heart ached for the hurt that snuck through her words. "People do a lot of good at this time of year too, you know."

"Yeah. I know. Sorry. And you're welcome. I'm just sorry that we got off to such a rocky start."

"Me too. Any chance you're free tonight?" Gabe shifted to get a better view of a flaming red cardinal at his feeder.

"Aren't you busy with the lights?"

"Yeah. But I was hoping you might come by, have some dinner, and then hang out for a while. If you aren't busy?" Did he just offer to cook? Gabe winced and crossed to the fridge. He scanned the shelves. If she didn't like spaghetti, they could always order in.

"I could do that. Can I bring something? Maybe pick up dinner? Do you even cook?"

"I do cook, in fact. But I haven't been to the grocery store lately, so unless you're in the mood for spaghetti, we can order in."

"I happen to love spaghetti. I'll bring dessert. What time?"

"Five? Go ahead and park out front. When you're ready to go, I'll stop the foot traffic for you."

He smiled as he ended the call and sent a quick text to Jake letting him know not to bother coming early. He'd do a quick run through of the lights and then get dinner started. How long would she stick around? There was the possibility of snow around nine. He'd love to watch it fall with her. But maybe she'd prefer to head home before then and avoid the inevitable road mess.

BEFORE HE REALIZED IT, the doorbell rang. Gabe frowned. He'd meant to go up and change into something nicer than his old plaid flannel. Too late now. He wiped his hands on a kitchen towel, tossed it over his shoulder, and strode to the door. One look at Tori and his heart stopped, then sped off, leaving him breathless.

She smiled. "Hi."

"Hi. Wow." His fingers itched to touch her, to twine through her hair. His lips warmed at the thought of pressing against hers. He cleared his throat. "Come on in. The spaghetti's nearly ready."

Tori stepped in and stopped. "I love your house. It's so easy to feel at home here. I noticed that the first time I came over. At the time, I didn't think it suited you. But now I can't imagine anything suiting you more."

Heat spread through him. Before he could stop himself, Gabe pulled Tori into his arms. He lowered his forehead to hers, the tips of their noses touching, and gazed into her eyes. "I'm so glad you could come tonight."

Her voice was breathy. "So am I."

With considerable effort, Gabe pulled himself back, though he kept a loose arm around her waist. "Let's go check on dinner."

"TELL ME YOUR FAVORITE CHRISTMAS MEMORY." Gabe threaded his fingers through Tori's as they walked through the snowman display toward the Nativity.

"I really don't have one. I have bad and not-quite-as-bad ones. But a favorite? Nope. What about you?"

Hmm. How did he choose? "I guess if I can only pick one, I'll go with the first Christmas after I became a believer. I'd always half-dreaded Christmas—caught up in finding all the right gifts, and worrying about guessing wrong, or what if I didn't get what I wanted. You know the drill. But that Christmas, we'd just gotten back from our first year on-site overseas and my parents were still alive. So I went home to visit, spend the holidays like usual. And the most amazing thing happened. I finally realized that Christmas is about gifts, sure, but not like we think of it. It's about Jesus coming to Earth—God's irreplaceable gift to us—and we celebrate by emulating his actions. So we give, not because we're hoping to win points or justify what we get in return, but because we've been so richly blessed, there's no possible response except to give back. That Christmas, I actually spent time with my parents and listened to their stories without having my mind on something else or trying to hurry them along so I could go do something I thought would be more fun. It ended up being the last Christmas we had together, and I'll always cherish it."

"That's lovely." Tori's voice was a murmur. "I just wish that sentiment didn't end when December twenty-sixth rolled around."

Gabe sighed. Wasn't there anything he could do to help her see the beauty of Christmas? "Isn't it enough that people embrace it for a little while? It opens the door to being able to share Christ with them, to remind them of the gifts they got and how desperately they pale in light of the gift God sent."

Tori turned to face him, her gaze searching his. "You really believe that, don't you? Not just in a superficial, ticket-to-heaven kind of way."

"I do."

12

Tori knocked on the frame of Ryan's office door. "Hey. Got a minute?"

Ryan leaned back in his chair, a furrow between his eyes. "I can take one."

"Thanks." Tori stepped in and closed the door behind her. Clutching her folder, she sat across from Ryan and fought the urge to clear her throat. Pitching stories wasn't new. But this one mattered. Plus...technically she was wrong not to have reported Geneva's contact the minute it came in. This could cost her job. "You know I wasn't happy to be assigned to the Robertson feature."

Ryan scoffed. "Understatement, but yes."

"After I finished the story, Geneva Stearns called me."

"Wait." Ryan lifted his fingers. "From the *Post*? That Geneva?"

Tori nodded.

Ryan scowled. "When was this?"

She hunched her shoulders. "A little over a week ago?"

"Go on." At least he'd only growled. No yelling. Or banging. Yet.

She swallowed the knot in her throat. "She wanted to know if I'd be willing to do a freelance article continuing her investigation from five years ago. Sort of a 'where are they now' kind of thing, but centered on Gabe and IA, Inc."

"And being an ethical employee of the *Trib*, you told her thanks but no and called your editor. Oh. Wait. That's *not* what happened."

"I know. I know, I'm sorry. Look." Tori twisted her hands in her lap. "I'm not proud of it, okay? I was having a hard time reconciling what I knew of Gabe from college with his current...altruism. But I did a little poking—just a tiny bit—and there's no basis for any investigation. Honestly, from what I can find, there was no basis for the investigation five years ago. I spoke with Geneva's primary source—"

This time Ryan did yell. And bang. "You what?"

Tori straightened her spine. It wasn't, technically, against the rules. Should she have handled it differently? Yes. But she was doing the right thing now. That should count for something. She forced her voice to remain steady and calm. "Can I finish? Please?"

He gave a curt nod.

"He's got sour grapes. It's an obvious case. He sold out of the company the first time things got hard and now he's bent out of shape that Gabe's doing well. I don't know what motivated him five years ago, but I'm pretty sure that's what's behind this new interest. Here." She tossed the folder on Ryan's desk. "These are my notes so far. I'd like permission to do the article, for the *Trib*, and show Gabe—and IA, Inc.—for the kind of company they are. A good company, run by good men, who do good deeds in the local community as well as providing necessary support to the military overseas."

Ryan flipped open the folder, lips pursed.

Tori waited while he paged through her notes. At least he

hadn't dismissed the idea out of hand. Maybe, just maybe, this would work.

He turned the last page and hummed. "Here's the thing, Gabe and I are old friends. I was part of the unit they were primarily attached to when they started out. We had some experiences together...that are best left alone. Point being, I won't see his name dragged through the mud."

"I'm not—"

"I can see that. But, I also don't think I can give the okay to the article given our friendship. It was one thing to highlight his Christmas display after he bought ad space. This is different." Ryan blew out a breath. "That said, I hate to think that Geneva's planning to do another story on him. She did such a hatchet job last time it nearly ruined them. Even though the accusations were spurious. What if you wrote the article for her?"

Tori frowned. "She wants another smear campaign though. I can't do that."

"If she thought she could get away with another unsupported story, she'd be writing it herself. She didn't bank on you doing more than cursory digging. Real investigative reporters don't cover the light displays."

Her lips twitched. "Isn't that what I told you?"

Ryan grinned. "In this case, it's a good thing I made you do it anyway. Take the week off, do the article—I can't let you use our resources here for another paper, but you have your own, right?"

She caught her lower lip between her teeth. She'd already used the easy sources. There was one she hadn't tapped yet. Her stomach sank. "I have someone."

"If you can figure out why Geneva's so determined to give Gabe a black eye it'd be a nice addition to the piece. Do you have to send it to Geneva first, or did you get an editor's contact info?"

"She gave me the editor. But she's asked to see my drafts."

Ryan shrugged. "Let her ask. When you get it done, send it straight to the editor, copy her if you want. They'll figure it out from there. If they say they're not going to run it, let me know and I'll shoot it up the chain to see if we can."

"Thanks, Ryan."

He handed her the folder. "Don't let me down, Victoria."

FOUR DAYS. Could she do this in four days? Christmas was Friday, she had to be back at work on Monday and ready to take on her regular duties for the *Trib*. As much as she might like to try and work within the confines of her sources here, the best bet—the sure bet—was to call Zane. Whether or not he'd help her remained to be seen. But she wasn't going to find out unless she picked up the phone.

"Here goes nothing, boys." She scrubbed each cat's head in turn and grabbed her cell, punching in her mother's number.

"Victoria, honey, how are you?" Beach music and muted conversation rumbled in the background of her mother's line.

"I'm good, thanks. How are the Caymans?"

"Just fantastic. Are you sure you can't make it out for a little while? There are so many handsome men down here, I'm sure you could find someone if you'd try."

"I still can't take the time off, Mom, sorry. Plus, I'm sort of seeing someone." She was, wasn't she? There had been several moments where she'd thought—hoped—Gabe might try to kiss her. Maybe it was too soon, having only been on two official dates, but surely it wasn't too soon to consider it a relationship?

"Really? Oh, that's wonderful. Tell me everything. Hang on, I'll go find someplace quieter."

"No, Mom, wait. Can I do that later? I actually called to talk to Zane."

"Zane? You want to talk to Zane? Why?"

Tori smiled at the bafflement in her mother's voice. She really hadn't made an effort to get to know her mother's new husband and she couldn't bear to call him her step father, but she could've at least been polite. "I have a favor to ask, actually, for a story I'm doing."

"Oh. Well, hang on and I'll get him. I'm sure he'd be happy to help."

Tori chewed her lip. She wouldn't have put money on his willingness to help. But she had to ask.

"Hey, Tori. What's up?"

"Hi, Zane. Um, I need a favor."

"Hit me."

That's it? He was just going to do it, no questions asked? She closed her eyes. How had she misjudged him so badly? And held onto it for so long. "First, I owe you an apology."

"Don't. If the situation was reversed, I'd probably be freaked out, too. To be honest, it was weird to fall in love with someone so much older than me, though don't tell your mom that. But she's an amazing woman and I'm lucky to have her. Now, what can I unearth for you with my amazing computer skills?"

She laughed and imagined him blowing across the tips of his fingers. "I have a list. Can I email it?"

13

W histling through his teeth, Gabe put his coffee mug and breakfast plate in the dishwasher. Three more nights of lights and then it was Christmas. He'd be closed on Christmas Day, but he'd run the lights on Saturday and Sunday nights for the few people who wanted to see them after Christmas was past. Then it'd be time to pack everything up and get back to business as usual. Even though the week between Christmas and New Year's was quiet, it'd be good to be back in the office on a more full-time basis. With Rick planning on heading to the States in February, Gabe needed to do a little rearranging of the schedule and make sure Rick's replacements were ready to go. February would be here before anyone realized it.

He checked the clock. Just after eight thirty on a Tuesday morning. She'd be at work already, wouldn't she? He grabbed his phone, pacing into the living room as it rang.

"Hello?" She sounded groggy.

"Hi, it's Gabe...did I wake you?"

"Yeah. Late night. Timezit?"

Gabe chuckled. "About eight thirty. Don't you have work?"

"Nah. Taking the week off. I was up late working on a free-lance project. What's up?"

"Well, I was wondering if you're free for lunch. I know we didn't have plans, but I was really hoping you'd swing by the lights last night. I missed you."

"Aww. I can do lunch. When and where?"

"Can I pick you up, say eleven?"

"Yeah, okay."

"See you then." Gabe hit end and tucked his phone in his pocket. Time to get to work on a little operation mistletoe of his own.

"THE MALL? Please tell me you're not seriously taking me to another mall. It's three days until Christmas." Tori crossed her arms, a frown etching her face.

Gabe laughed and accelerated down the row of the parking garage as he spied an empty spot. "Come on, it'll be fun. Plus, there's the best little restaurant in here. Even if it is the mall."

"At least it's the fancy mall. I never come to this one. If I come into Tyson's, I go across the street."

"See? It'll be a new experience then." Gabe turned off the engine and bumped her elbow with his. "What could possibly go wrong?"

She snickered. "Now you're just asking for it."

They wandered through one of the huge department stores that was intended to be a draw to the mall overall, dodging the overzealous perfume salespeople. Gabe grabbed Tori's hand and pulled her to his side as he stopped to view the map. Even expecting the jolt, it wired his system into overdrive.

"I want to make one quick stop on our way to lunch."

Tori's stomach rumbled. "All right. A short stop?"

"Most likely." He gave her hand a tug. "This way."

"It's not as crowded as I expected." Tori glanced around. There were people rushing from store to store, but it wasn't packed by any stretch of the imagination.

"Upscale mall, like you said. I'm guessing across the street is busier." Gabe stepped onto the down escalator. "Still, they really know how to decorate here. As far as I'm concerned, it wins compared to all the area malls."

Tori pursed her lips. "I can see that. I don't have a ton of comparison data, mind you. But the mall in Ballston tries, but they're nowhere near this level of glitz without being gaudy. That said, I'll take online shopping any day of the week. Free shipping and no piped-in music. Can't be beat."

He shook his head. "But then you miss out on experiences like this."

"Like wh...no way."

"Oh, come on. He doesn't bite." Gabe eyed the Santa sitting on a golden chair with plush red velvet cushions. "I'll go first if that helps."

"You're serious? You're a thirty-year-old and you're going to sit on Santa's lap?"

"Twenty-eight, same as you. And yeah, that's the plan. It'll be fun." He grinned and pulled her into the short line.

Tori muttered under her breath as they waited for three sets of moms and toddlers to have their turn.

"Ho ho ho! Merry Christmas!" Santa patted his leg. "You're never too old to believe in Santa Claus. Come and have a seat."

Gabe winked at Tori and perched on the man's knee, whispering in his ear. The elf behind the camera called for their attention and snapped two shots. Gabe stood, accepted his candy cane, and pointed at Tori. "Your turn."

"This is so dumb." She stomped over to Santa and sat. "I'm sorry about this. He's...incorrigible."

Santa laughed. "I'm not supposed to share Christmas wishes with anyone other than the elves, but your friend there? All he asked for was for you to have a good one this year."

Gabe waited as the elf behind the camera snapped photos of Tori. When she reached him, she leaned up and pecked his cheek. "You're sweet. But this is still ridiculous."

Heat spread out from where her lips touched. "Ridiculous or not, we have to wait a minute so I can buy our prints."

14

Tori was still grinning about lunch when Bernie and Woodsie started clamoring for their dinner. She glanced at the photo of Gabe on Santa's lap sitting on her coffee table in the cardboard frame the mall provided. Sweet man. She'd planned to take her print, come home, and toss it. But he'd insisted that her photo was for him and the other way around. After lunch, they'd strolled through more of the mall, looking at the elaborate Christmas displays. How did he manage to enjoy all the trappings that the culture put on this season and keep his eyes so firmly focused on the real reason behind the celebration? She wanted that ability in her own life.

After scooping kibble for the boys and fixing a peanut butter and jelly sandwich for herself, Tori went back to her laptop. Zane had come through with some good information, but there was still nothing on Geneva that explained her desire to torpedo Gabe's company. Could it just be random? That seemed unlikely. But if Zane, with the resources of his computer security firm, couldn't find anything...maybe there was nothing to find.

Her email chimed.

Tori brushed the crumbs off her fingers and switched to her inbox. She skimmed the email from Zane, a smile tugging at the corner of her mouth. He'd come through. Big time. Switching to her word processing article, she began to type.

At two in the morning, Tori shut the lid of her laptop. She'd sent the article to the editor, with a copy to Geneva Stearns as a courtesy. It didn't seem likely that Geneva would be grateful. She rubbed her eyes. Didn't matter. Reporters were supposed to be committed to the truth, and even if they wrote for a publication with a preferred spin, they still needed facts to back up their stories. Not personal bias. Maybe nothing would come of it, but she'd done her part and could rest easy.

TORI FUMBLED for her cell phone, grumbling under her breath. She really needed to remember to put the thing on silent before bed. Then maybe she'd be allowed to sleep in instead of getting early wakeup calls. She squinted at the clock as she answered. Almost ten. Okay, maybe not so early. Still.

"Hello?"

"Victoria Spencer?"

She should've checked the caller ID. "Yes?"

"This is Martin Harrison at the *Post*. I'm calling about the article you submitted."

"What can I do for you?"

He cleared his throat. "I've been in a meeting with Geneva Stearns for most of the morning. She says this isn't the article she asked you to write."

Tori fought a laugh. "No, I don't imagine it's what she expected. But all she requested was that I look into Intelligence Associates, Inc. as a follow-up to her article several years ago. I did that and I reported my findings."

"Hmm. Geneva is fairly emphatic that your story is completely fabricated."

"She would be. But if you do your research, you'll find the same things I did. The first support mission IA performed uncovered two leaks in the operation, and the reporter embedded with the unit was one of them. He was sending his stories and information directly to Geneva. When he got caught, her source dried up, and if you look at her financial records, you'll see her income took a pretty big hit at the same time." Tori fought to keep her voice calm even though her heart was pounding.

"And you got her financial information, how?"

"From a source of my own. All perfectly legal."

Seconds ticked by before Martin spoke again. "We'll have to look into this. However, if we can verify your findings, expect the article to run on Friday."

"That's Christmas."

"Ms. Spencer, as an aspiring investigative reporter you ought to know the news cycle never sleeps. And this, if true, is news. I'll be in touch."

Tori hit 'end' and sank back against her pillows, her heart rate slowly settling back to normal. She was going to have an article published in the *Post*. She squealed and drummed her heels against the mattress before bouncing out of bed. She had a boyfriend, of sorts. And things were starting to finally smooth out between her and her mom. Maybe this was the year her Christmas curse would be broken.

"I'm so glad you were free." Tori pushed off Gabe's porch with one toe and got the swing going. "Even if you need to be here for the delivery guys."

He slipped his arm around her shoulder. "You brought

lunch. Besides, it's a nice enough day, we might actually hit fifty if that sun keeps poking through the clouds."

She grinned. Maybe it was too chilly to sit and swing on the porch, but it felt right. Cozy. "Two more days 'til Christmas. Are you ready?"

"I'm expecting a few last minute gifts in the mail today or tomorrow, but otherwise, yeah. You?"

Tori lifted a shoulder. "I guess. I don't really have anyone I shop for. I bought myself a new sweater, it's in my closet waiting for Friday to be worn, but otherwise, there's not much to do."

"You don't send gifts to your parents? Siblings?"

Her stomach twisted. She'd tried that for several years, but it was more trouble than it was worth. "Not anymore. Dad tries to make it feel like I'm part of his new family, but the reality is I'm just not. He and his new wife have their own kids and there's simply no room for me. He sends presents and makes the offer for me to tag along, but I know better than to say yes. Couple of years ago, he mentioned how they and the kids have so much and really don't need any more clutter. So I buy chickens or something for a family in Africa and send them a note letting them know it was done in their name. Mom and Zane are pretty much the same. My taste isn't extravagant enough for Mom, so she always wants to know where I got things, the subtext is so that she can return it. So they get chickens or whatever, too. Less than ten minutes online and I'm done."

He frowned and rubbed her shoulder. "That's sad. I'm sorry."

Tori laid her head on his arm and let him soothe her. "I'm okay with it. Mostly."

"So what will you do Christmas Day? If you don't give them gifts, you're clearly not spending the day with family either."

She gave the swing another little push. "I usually go to the movies. It's not super crowded and there are always a few good new releases this time of year to take up part of the day. Then I come home and make a turkey breast for me and the cats. It's not as depressing as it sounds."

He laughed. "I guess it's good you realize it sounds depressing. You met Jake."

Where was that going? "Um. Yeah?"

"He and a few other friends are coming over, everyone's bringing something to share, we'll do a big white elephant exchange. You should come."

She hadn't even checked to see what movies were showing yet. Jake seemed nice enough, if a tad obnoxious. But spending more time with Gabe would be nice. "I think I'd like that."

"Cool. Anytime after eleven. We try to eat around 2. Don't spend more than ten bucks on the gift, and we don't do the nice white elephant game. Get something tacky."

15

Gabe checked his watch. People should be here any minute. Would Tori show? He'd talked to her, briefly, on Wednesday and Thursday, but she'd been busy editing her freelance assignment and not able to get away. Not even for a quick meal. But she'd be here today. She hadn't said she wouldn't...so she would. And so would Jake, Angel, and a lot of the rest of the crew from work who either didn't have family nearby and didn't feel like travelling or had spouses who were deployed. There were a lot of military spouses working behind the scenes at IA.

"Knock knock." Jake strolled into the kitchen and set a bakery box on the counter. "The door was open, so I figured I could just come on in."

"That is, in fact, why I left it open. Plus, it's practically spring out there today. I thought they were saying we were in for a cold snap."

Jake shrugged. "You know weather guys just throw darts at random words to make up their forecasts. Besides, winter doesn't really come to D.C. until January."

"True enough. Feel like running down to the chest freezer in the basement and grabbing a bag of ice for the cooler?"

"Sure." Jake headed toward the stairs. "Need anything else while I'm down there?"

"Don't think so. Thanks, man." Gabe peeked in the oven. The prime rib was crisping nicely. They were still on track for eating right at two.

The doorbell rang. Gabe wiped his hands on a towel and tossed it on the counter as he strode to the door. Not everyone took the hint like Jake did. Though Jake was here so much, it was like his second home. His heart leapt when he saw Tori shifting from one foot to the other on the porch, her arms full with a huge box wrapped in silver paper with acres of curly ribbon bursting off the top of it and a precariously balanced casserole dish.

"You came. Let me help you with that." Gabe reached for the box.

She nudged the casserole with her chin. "Just grab that. The box isn't heavy. Just big."

He eyed the box as he took the warm food. "Stick it under the tree. I promise not to tell who brought what. It's part of the host code."

Tori laughed. "I didn't realize there was one, but it's good to know."

"Does this need to be refrigerated?"

"Should be okay. We can reheat it before we eat, right?" Tori looked up from placing the box near the tree.

He nodded and jerked his head toward the kitchen as he headed in that direction. "Of course."

Gabe slid the dish onto the counter and turned, practically bumping into Tori as she walked and rooted around in her enormous purse at the same time.

She pulled a wrapped cylinder out and handed it to him. "Merry Christmas."

"Are we doing gifts now? I was hoping maybe you'd stay after everyone left and we could do them then."

Her eyebrows lifted. Had she not expected him to get her something? "Okay. Just set it aside."

"Hey, Tori." Jake clomped up the stairs with a bag of ice slung over his shoulder. "Glad you could make it. Christmas with Gabe is always a good time. Where's the cooler?"

Gabe pointed.

"Can I help with anything?" Tori crossed her arms and looked uncomfortable.

"Want to man the door? Then I can keep an eye on things in here. You know where the gifts go, they can bring food on back. But you'll be held to the host code, too."

Tori chuckled. "I can do that."

EVERY CHRISTMAS with the gang was fun, but this year it seemed to be more...everything. It had to be Tori. She was like a bright light on the far side of the room. It was interesting to watch her. She had a ready laugh and a quick comeback when teasing worked its way to her, but for the most part, she hovered on the edge of the crowd, watching. Was that the reporter in her? She hadn't been like that before. At least not that he'd noticed. In fact, Gabe never would have pegged her as having any introverted tendencies at all with the way she'd barged back into his life. And then gone snooping around the company. Had she really thought he wouldn't hear about it?

"You in there?" Jake plopped onto the sofa and jabbed Gabe in the side with his elbow.

"Yeah. Just watching, trying to figure out who'll be the first to say they have to go. That always seems to start an avalanche. And as much as I know everyone comes because they don't want to spend the day on their own, I also know there are other places for many of them to be." Gabe turned to Jake. "Even you."

Jake snickered. "Busted. I might actually win the break-up-the-party prize. I promised one of the older families at church that I'd be there for a late supper. I remind them of their son. He never made it home from Afghanistan. Christmas, especially, is tough."

Gabe clapped his friend on the shoulder. "Go. They need you more than we do."

"You sure? I can stretch it another hour. They're not the only ones who have trouble being alone on Christmas."

Gabe looked across the room at Tori and his whole body warmed. "I don't think it's going to be as big a problem this year as it has been."

"Hmm. Be careful, man. Don't forget she's a reporter." Jake stood.

Gabe frowned. They were past that, weren't they? The time they'd spent together...he couldn't be the only one feeling the connection. "I don't think there's anything to worry about."

Jake gave him a long look then turned his attention to the room. "I hate to be the one to do it, but I've got to run. It was good to see everyone outside the office. And I'll look forward to seeing you all back *in* the office on Monday."

Groans and laughter followed Jake's comment. And, as Gabe had expected, others started to gather their coats and dishes and make their exits. Within thirty minutes, only Tori remained.

"I stashed your gift behind the tree. Hopefully...yeah, here it is." Gabe grinned as he wrestled the skinny rectangle out of the branches. "There's always the concern that it'll end up being mistaken for a white elephant gift. Usually if it's hard to get out from behind the tree, people realize they're not supposed to grab it."

Tori chuckled and reached for her purse. "That's why I just

tucked yours back into my bag. I didn't want it going astray...you didn't spend a lot, right? Cause this is more of a token...and that looks important."

"Homemade. Promise." Gabe drew an X over his heart and handed her the package. "You go first."

Her mouth opened then closed on a sigh. She offered him the tube and settled his gift on her lap, resting a hand on top of it. "Thanks for inviting me today. This was the nicest Christmas I've had in a really long time."

He scooted so their knees touched and leaned in, closing some of the distance between them. What would it be like to brush his lips across hers? Every nerve ending in his body was on fire. It'd be so easy to lean forward just a little more and find out. Her gaze locked onto his. Without another thought, he eased forward, her breath a whisper of air that mingled with his own before their lips met and electricity sizzled through him. He wanted more.

Tori cupped his cheek before her hands slid around his neck, her fingers tangling in his hair. He swallowed and forced himself to break the kiss. He was a new creation. The old had gone. But oh, how the old wanted to come back.

"Merry Christmas."

Her laugh was just the tiniest bit frantic. "Is that part of the present?"

Gabe ran his thumb over her lower lip. "For me, definitely. I've been thinking about doing that for a while now."

"I did a lot of that kind of thinking in college." Tori's hand flew to her mouth, her eyes wide. "Oh. Tell me I didn't say that out loud."

He cocked his head to the side, one corner of his mouth tugging up. He'd had no idea. Or he'd been too full of himself to realize it. "Maybe we should do it again, make up for lost opportunities?"

"No. I want to open my present." She put her hand on his

chest and pushed him back before tearing open the wrapping paper.

Gabe watched as she uncovered the painting. Would she remember it? In college, he'd told her he threw it away, but he'd never been able to. It wasn't the self-portrait he'd turned in for a grade, just a sketch of Tori in class he'd done while tuning out the professor. He'd dug it out of his box of college junk, transferred it to a canvas, and filled in with paint.

"I'm still not incredibly artistic. But it's how I remember you."

"You...I...this is...wow." Tori pressed her lips to his, pulling back as he reached for her. "I love it. And now I'm embarrassed. I didn't...let me get you a real present. That's just..."

Gabe held her present out of reach as she grabbed for it. "No way. It's Christmas. You brought me a gift, I'm opening it. That's how this works."

She hunched her shoulders, her expression pained. "It's really nothing. Not compared to this. This is wonderful and that...just isn't."

"I'm sure it's great." He winked and ripped open the wrapping. The newspaper inside uncurled, revealing the headline NERVES OF STEEL, HEART OF GOLD just above the press photo of Gabe that showed him by the Intelligence Associates reception desk. He swallowed, his stomach churning. Mouth dry, he managed something between a whisper and a croak, "What is this?"

16

The fuzzy warmth that was floating through her vanished. Tori looked at Gabe. Scarcely controlled anger pulsed off of him. What was going on? Her mouth was suddenly dry.

"I...I thought you'd be happy. It's good PR, exposure to a much bigger audience. It mentions the light display...Gabe, what's wrong?"

He carefully laid the newspaper aside, his movements measured and precise. "If I'd wanted an article in the *Post*, I would've approached the *Post*, not the *Tribune*. And if I'd wanted the employee benevolence fund to be public knowledge, I would've listed it among the benefits on our jobs page online."

She winced. "I know. And I tried to leave it out, but I needed to show that you're so much more—the company is so much more—than the carrion crows that Geneva Stearns painted you as in her first article. She was trying to do it again. Her and Hewitt Michaels."

"Hewitt?" Gabe frowned, shaking his head. "I'd always

wondered if Hewitt was part of the first hatchet job that woman did on IA. But this...what possessed you to do this?"

Tori curled her fingers around the edge of the painting in her lap. At least he didn't sound like he was trying not to scream anymore. But he didn't look anything like the man who'd kissed her a few minutes ago. "After the lights article ran in the *Trib*, Geneva approached me about doing a follow up. I had some...let's go with hard feelings from college still to deal with so I agreed. But getting to know you, researching IA, I realized I had an opportunity to set the record straight. You deserve that. You're a good man, Gabe, and you do good things for so many people. Why don't you want everyone to know?"

The muscles in his jaw bunched. He drew in a long breath through his nose. "I think you should leave."

Tears burned in the back of her eyes, but Tori nodded and stood, still clutching the painting. She wouldn't give him the satisfaction of seeing her cry. She grabbed her purse and fled toward the door. With her hand on the knob, she turned. "I'm sorry."

He scoffed and shook his head. "Right."

SHE MADE IT HOME. That in itself was something of a Christmas miracle, since she'd been unable to hold back the tears once she made it off Gabe's porch. Clad in flannel pajamas, she curled up on the couch and let her cats comfort her.

"Eleven years running, guys. I think I can safely say Christmas is not my holiday. Maybe it spreads love and goodwill everywhere else, but I just can't seem to catch a break."

Woodward gave a sympathetic *prrrow* before jumping off the couch and scampering into the kitchen. Bernstein just looked at her, flicking the tip of his tail.

Her phone chimed with an incoming text.

With a sigh, Tori snagged her phone off the coffee table and swiped the screen. The text was a photo of her mom and Zane on the beach in swimsuits and Santa hats. She tried to work up a smile, but failed. She texted back a Merry Christmas wish, then, since it was there, texted her dad and Ryan as well. Might as well let people think she was having a good time. Like a normal person.

After a few minutes, Ryan texted back: *Nice job on the article in the Post. See you back at work on Monday. Right?*

Was he really worried? She sent an affirmative and powered down her phone. Though the editor at the *Post* had been willing to run the article after he'd done the fact checking, he'd been justifiably annoyed that Geneva had done such a shoddy job in the first place. And, more, that Tori had made it inescapably clear. Even if Geneva got canned, as she should for fabricating a story and profiting from leaked intelligence, Martin wasn't likely to come knocking on her door anytime soon. She flipped on the television and switched to the station that ran the leg lamp movie back-to-back all day long. Maybe the little boy and his Christmas duck could get her mind off the fact that she'd torpedoed her chance at anything with Gabe, trying to do right by him.

17

Gabe turned off the snow blower as Jake pulled into the driveway. "You're late."

Jake rubbed his hands together and stuffed them in the pockets of his coat. "Dock my pay."

With a chuckle, Gabe pushed the blower toward the garage. "I finished clearing all the paths and the area down by the Nativity and snack shack already. It's a powdery snow, so it was easy. How was dinner last night?"

"Oh, you know the Morrisons, don't you? They're great. She made way too much food, so my freezer is stuffed. Hopefully it'll keep when I head back out. At least 'til Rick gets here." Jake leaned against the grill of his truck. "February, right?"

Gabe nodded, considering. "Maybe I should head over at the end of the month, do a little new year evaluation on-site. You could hold down the fort, get a chance to eat through that food."

"No way." Jake pushed off the truck and crossed the driveway. Gabe angled the snow blower into its space and frowned. "What's going on?"

"Nothing. It was just an idea."

"Not buying it." Jake narrowed his eyes. "Maybe I'm the one who should be asking how the rest of your evening went."

Gabe groaned and kicked the snow blower's wheel. "Don't you read the paper?"

"You know better than that." Jack grinned. "The less I know, the happier I am. I get all the info I need from our mission briefings and social media. If something interests me enough that I want to form an opinion, I'll do a little digging. Otherwise? The only thing I get out of reading the paper is an unquenchable urge to crawl into a dark room and sleep for fifty years."

Gabe raked a hand through his hair. How his friend managed to work in intelligence with that attitude was a question for the ages. Though maybe there was something to it. "Come on inside. I've got the coffee pot on."

Jake's eyebrows lifted but he remained mute.

Gabe toed off his boots in the tiny mud room that led from the garage into the kitchen. Sock-footed, he crossed to the recycling bin and dug out the paper Tori had given him. He tossed it on the kitchen table and strode to the coffee pot. "This was her Christmas gift to me."

Jake craned his neck as he looked at the paper. Frowning, he dropped into a chair and shifted the article to a better angle. He glanced up with a tight smile as Gabe set a steaming mug of coffee in front of him.

Gabe watched for a reaction—any reaction. Jake was hands down the most even-tempered of the three founders. Between Rick and Gabe it was pretty evenly matched, but Jake tended to take things in stride. Surely, though, this would get him going. "Well?"

Jake shrugged.

"That's it? A shrug?"

He sighed. "You know I've never understood your deep desire for secrecy when it comes to how we help out our employees. They're family to us. And family helps out when it's needed. So we just do. And given how they included your light display and OM? You're going to have record crowds—and donations, most likely—tonight. I just don't see the downside."

"That's 'cause it's not your face and name plastered across the top half of the page." Gabe stalked to the sink and dumped out the coffee that had turned bitter and was twisting his stomach in knots. It had to be the coffee. It couldn't be Jake's reaction.

"I don't know about that. I'm mentioned. So's Rick. Hewitt's even in there." Jake offered a vulpine grin. "Though his mention isn't what I'd term complimentary. Accurate, though. And still, I'm not seeing the big deal. What'd you say to Tori?"

"I asked her to go."

Jake stared open-mouthed for a long second, scoffed, and shook his head. "You're an idiot."

"How do you get that?" Gabe set his mug in the sink and turned, arms crossed.

"Why do you do this every year?" Jake pointed toward the light display.

"You know why." What did that have to do with anything?

"Humor me."

Gabe scowled. Fine. Whatever. "Because Christmas is an amazing reminder of the depth and breadth of God's love for us. It's forgiveness and redemption all rolled together into the tiny human package of Jesus. And you get it, almost immediately, when you stop and really think about Christmas, even if you grew up with it just being a crazy day of gifts and family."

"And?"

What did he mean? "What are you getting at?"

"You're the one who's always going on about how Christmas is just the beginning, but the real change of heart that comes from Jesus is something that manifests every day in the little things. Like our employee program, for example. And this article captures that. So I guess I don't understand why the central message of everything you believe being put out there for a wider audience than you imagined possible upsets you."

Gabe drew in a breath and held it. Jake wasn't wrong. But it still didn't sit right. "Because it's not supposed to be about me. Or IA. It's just Jesus. He's the only one I want people thinking about. That article is going to have people painting me as some kind of philanthropist and putting the company on the 'best places to work' lists."

"Oh, sure. I can see how that's a terrible, terrible thing. We should look into suing."

Gabe scrubbed a hand over his face. "Be sarcastic if you want, but you won't be here to field the calls and do the interviews."

"Price of leadership, man." Jake stood and tapped the paper. "This is a good Christmas present, and you owe Tori an apology."

GABE FUMED throughout the evening's light show. It didn't help that the article doubled the crowd. At least. If it kept up all weekend, he'd be a fool not to stay open until New Year's. All the bigger displays did that, taking advantage of folks who were off work between the holidays, and government employees who, even if they didn't actually take the time off, worked considerably reduced hours because none of the higher ups were in. One part of him toyed with sticking to the original plan, but a peek in the donation bucket half-way through the night silenced the spiteful part of his brain. Another week and he could probably double, maybe triple, what he'd made for Operation Mistletoe during the rest of the month.

Jake's snarky comments over the walkie talkie had, at least, been entertaining. But his parting shot had crossed a line. 'Do the right thing.' Isn't that what he was doing? Oh sure, Jake had meant regarding Tori. Gabe got that. But the right thing? It wasn't a simple, clear-cut answer. She knew how he felt about publicity. It was one thing to highlight the Christmas lights. She'd done that for the *Trib*, after all. But to delve into the company? And their employee benefits? Angel had told him about her probing there, but had also assured him that Tori understood it wasn't for the public record. And now it was.

Gabe hit the master switch, shutting off the lights for night. It was just after midnight. And he was never going to get to sleep.

18

Tori sank into the hot tub on the balcony of her father's ski condo and stared out over the lit slopes. He'd seemed surprised when she emailed and asked if there was any way she could use the place over the weekend, but since they were cruising this year, it wasn't as if they needed it. In the end, he'd arranged it with the management company and she'd jumped in the car for the not-quite three-hour drive after setting up the cats' auto-feeder. They'd be fine for a couple of days and she...just needed to get away.

Why had she thought this Christmas was going to be any different?

That was a path that was better to leave alone. And yet, her thoughts kept straying in that direction. Gabe. Drat the man. A full twenty-four hours later and just thinking about his kisses made her lips tingle. And she couldn't even dismiss it as simple chemistry. Not that it wasn't chemistry. No, it wasn't *just* chemistry. She liked him as a person, too. And that made it more complicated. Maybe they weren't friends yet, but they'd been on their way. Losing that was worse than missing out on his kisses for the rest of her life. Add in the fact that she couldn't very well go back to Pastor Brown's church, regardless of how much she'd liked it there, and she was three for three in the loss department.

All things being equal, this might be the worst Christmas yet.

She sank lower, letting the hot, bubbling water close over her shoulders. Maybe tomorrow she'd hit the slopes, see if she had any skiing ability left. She hadn't been since she broke her leg, but there was no medical reason she couldn't try it again. And wasn't that what you were supposed to do after you got knocked down? Or did that just make you a glutton for punishment?

TORI FROWNED as her cell began a series of beeps. She moved away from the start of the slope she'd been about to tackle and, using her teeth, tugged off a glove and fished the phone out of her pocket.

Where are you?

Hadn't Ryan gotten her email? She'd sent it last night after deciding to stay one more day. Her Sunday excursions onto the mountain went better than she'd anticipated. Though she'd never be a world-class skier, she could hold her own on something beyond the bunny slope. And she'd been able to reconnect with God. Long stretches on some of the less-crowded off-road trails were perfect for prayer and introspection. Who knew? Maybe she didn't know what to do about Gabe, if anything, but she was ready to rediscover her faith.

Tori tapped out a quick reply and hit send. Two seconds later, the phone rang.

"You're supposed to let me know when you take a day."

She groaned. "I sent you an email. That's always been enough in the past."

"And an email would've been fine, if you'd sent it." Ryan's voice was edged with something she couldn't identify. Concern, maybe? But why?

"Hang on, I'll pull it up in my sent folder and forward it to you. Maybe the spam filters are acting up again. And really...why does it matter? You have a knitting bee you've decided to have me cover?" Tori swiped open her email app and scrolled through her sent file. Where was it? She'd sent it right after dinner. A bold number caught her eye. Outbox. "Augh. It didn't go through. It's sitting here in my outbox."

"Aha." Now he sounded smug.

"Sorry. There. Now it's on its way. What's going on, Ryan?" The text she'd sent should've been enough. For him to call was weird.

"Nothing. I just wanted to make sure you're all right. That we'd see you tomorrow."

"I'll be there. I'm heading back after lunch. You don't have to worry. One article in the *Post* hasn't sent hordes of papers to my door begging me to work for them. Besides, I'm not convinced it's worth the hassle."

"What do you mean?"

She blew out a breath. "Don't worry about it. Just be happy I have a newfound respect for small papers, okay? I'll see you tomorrow; it's too cold to be standing still out here."

"All right. Be careful."

Tori rolled her eyes and hit end before zipping the phone back into her jacket pocket. She tugged her glove back on, adjusted her sunglasses, and headed toward the start of the trail. With any luck, she'd be able to get in five or six runs before it was time to head home.

∼

TORI DROPPED into her office chair and booted up her computer. After a week off, there was no telling how much internal email she'd have to wade through. Why couldn't they let her load it on her phone? Every time she asked, she got some sort of bureaucratic run around about security, but if the government could manage it, why couldn't they?

"You're back."

She swiveled in her chair and smiled at Ryan. "So it seems. Did I miss anything?"

"Nope. You busy New Year's Eve?"

Her eyebrows shot up. "Does your wife know you're asking other women out?"

"Ha ha. We had an event crop up." He held up a hand. "I know, I know, you don't do fluff pieces, but everyone else is already double or triple booked. And we really have to cover this."

Her vision of spending the evening in pajamas on her couch with her cats watching movies until midnight evaporated. She could say no. Probably. But... "I guess I have plans now."

Ryan grinned. "Great. I'll send you the details as soon as I have them."

"What do you mean? New Year's Eve is tomorrow."

He nodded. "I know. They're just firming up a few details. It's not 'til night anyway."

Tori growled and stood, hobbling after him. "Don't make me chase you all the way to your office."

Ryan stopped, his gaze flicking down at her feet. "What did you do?"

"It's just a sprain..."

"Didn't I tell you to be careful? Maybe skiing isn't your sport."

Tori waved it away, heat crawling up her neck onto her face. "It's fine. I wasn't skiing."

"But you went to—"

"Yeah, I know. And I did ski. Look, I tripped over boots someone left in the middle of the floor in the lodge, okay?"

Ryan laughed. "Only you, Victoria. Lucky for you, the event tomorrow's casual. You can wear sneakers if you need to."

Tori watched as he walked off, still chuckling. Something about this assignment wasn't sitting right. But there was no point trying to get answers out of Ryan until he was ready.

19

"Okay, I did my part. She'll be here tomorrow night." Ryan held the Styrofoam cup of coffee in both hands. "I'm still amazed there are this many people out tonight. It's cold."

Gabe ignored the jitterbug that started up in his stomach. "How badly did you have to threaten her to get her to agree?"

"She doesn't know where she's going yet. She's just agreed to the article. I'll tell her when it's too late to back out or try to switch."

Gabe winced. That wasn't quite what he had in mind. This was going to backfire. Badly. "Maybe..."

"Trust me. I know Victoria. If you want to get her back out here, this is the only way I see it happening. Plus, you want the check presentation in the paper, right? Two birds, one stone." Ryan shrugged and took a sip.

"But not if she's here under false pretenses. I need to apologize to her...I want...I..."

"Have it bad." Ryan shook his head. "Been there, done that. Though I'm pretty sure I didn't mess things up quite as badly with Ellie when we were dating."

It was true. Ryan and Ellie had one of those relationships that seemed destined for smooth sailing from day one. "Yeah, well. Not everyone's as lucky as you are."

"Or as bullheaded as you."

Gabe frowned. "Whose side are you on?"

"Both. Look, man, Tori's great. She has some, let's call it 'assertiveness issues' sometimes. But with her, life will never be boring. And of all the guys I know, you're the first one I can think of who can handle her."

That was something, at least. He'd gone by Tori's place over the weekend to try and talk to her, even looked for her at church on the off chance that she'd give Pastor Brown another try. He finally broke down and called Ryan Sunday night and found out she was out of town. It was so much better to know that than to think she was ignoring him. And that was a revelation.

"I just hope she'll give me a chance."

Ryan slapped Gabe on the shoulder. "'Tis the season."

New Year's Eve. Gabe stared out the kitchen window as the first fingers of sunrise poked through the trees, shooting diamonds of light off the frost-covered Christmas lights. Tonight was it. The last night of the year. Last night of the display. Was it also his last chance with Tori?

The Executive Director of Operation Mistletoe was coming for the check presentation at eight p.m. He'd toyed with doing it at midnight, but who wanted to spend New Year's Eve outside? Well, other than the crazy people in New York City. People would still stop by, but they could do it on their way to whatever parties they were attending. And maybe if everyone took off afterward, and the crowd thinned, he could close early.

Maybe Tori would stay and they could ring in the New Year together.

He was getting ahead of himself. But the possibility was energizing.

Gabe spent the morning converting the choir risers into a platform by the Nativity. It was a good place to present the donation check, remind everyone what this was all about. By noon, it was good enough. He headed inside to get lunch and start working on a tear-down plan for the display. As much as he loved doing this every year, it was time to get his yard back. And have evenings free to spend inside by the fire. Especially since it appeared that winter was finally settling down to stay for a while.

"I brought subs." Jake looked up from the kitchen table and pushed at a wrapped oval.

"Make yourself at home." Gabe crossed to the sink to wash his hands. "When'd you get here?"

"Dunno. Five, ten minutes? You set for tonight?"

"I am now. Thanks for all your help."

Jake snickered. "Hey, I brought you lunch. I could've waited 'til five like you said."

This was true. And it'd help pass the afternoon to have Jake around. He'd be heading back to their overseas office next week and Gabe would be back to running things at work without the benefit of a good friend nearby. Not that he didn't have good people in this office, but they weren't his pals. Not like Jake and Rick. "Okay, you get a pass. What kind?"

"Meatball."

Gabe's stomach rumbled. "Good choice. It's stinkin' cold out there today. And that wind. I'll be surprised if we have many people come out. I wouldn't if I didn't have to."

"Think Tori'll come?"

Gabe opened the paper wrapper and poked a meatball. Still somewhat warm. Good enough. He lifted half for a bite. Would

Tori come? "Ryan said she accepted the assignment. But she didn't know—maybe still doesn't—that it's here. Knowing her, she might still work out a way to swap with someone."

"Been praying about it?" Jake grabbed the pepper grinder from the center of the table and added a liberal dose to his meal.

"Yeah. Though I still don't have a ton of direction. I know an apology is the first step. But after that...I miss her. It's only been a week and it's like there's this gaping hole where my heart's supposed to be."

Jake's eyebrows lifted. "That's not direction?"

"I don't know. Is it direction or infatuation?"

"Why can't it be both? Relationships have to start somewhere. You like her, you have good conversations with her. So there's some kind of friendship, right? You're not simply thinking of her looks or trying to get her into bed."

"That's not who I am anymore, man, you know that."

"Yeah, I do. Do you?" Jake stood and went into the kitchen. He took a glass out of the cupboard and filled it at the sink. "It's okay to be attracted to someone, particularly when you're attracted to all of her, not just her body. Somewhere along the line, I think you got mixed up about that."

Had he? "I just don't want to fall into that trap again. Isn't it better to be cautious?"

"Cautious, yes. Immobile? Maybe not so much."

Gabe rubbed the back of his neck. Jake might be harsh, but he wasn't wrong. "So, what? What's that mean I should do?"

"Tell her how you feel. Put your cards on the table and see what happens."

20

Tori fumed as she paced her living room. It was almost seven. How was she supposed to get to her assignment on time if she didn't know where to go? She checked her phone. Ryan had been dodging her calls all day. There was no other word for it. She'd tried calling his office, his cell, even the main switchboard of the paper, though she hadn't really expected to get anyone there. If she'd had his home number, she would've tried that. What was going on?

Her phone chimed with an incoming text. An address...in Clifton? No. Absolutely not. She hit the call button. He'd better pick up...

"That was fast."

"Absolutely not, Ryan. Whatever Gabe is up to for New Year's, he can do in the presence of another reporter."

"I told you, there isn't anyone else free. Come on, it's a one-hour ceremony, tops. You can manage that, can't you?"

"It's not a matter of managing it. Beyond the awkwardness, there's no way he wants me there. And it's just...not a good idea." Her voice broke. Tori balled her hands into fists. She wasn't going to cry over him anymore. He'd made himself clear.

She'd get over it. If anything, she owed him some thanks for getting her back to God. But other than that—it was time for a clean break.

"What if I told you that he asked me to get you out there. You, Tori. By name."

"Why? So he can rub it in?"

Ryan's sigh crackled in her ear. "No. Because he misses you. And he's sorry."

"He couldn't pick up the phone himself?"

"Would you have answered?"

Probably not. Going from sizzling kisses in the glow of the Christmas tree to being told to leave still had her head spinning if she dwelt on it. "Fine. I'll go. But I'm leaving after the ceremony—what is it?"

"Check presentation to Operation Mistletoe. They brought in almost four times what they were able to do last year. I think most of that is in the last week. Because of your article in the *Post*. He knows that, too. Can I give you one piece of unsolicited advice?"

She sighed. "Why not?"

"Give him a chance."

$\sim$

TORI MERGED into the steady trickle of people walking from the nearby parking area to Gabe's house. Attendance was higher than she expected. Didn't they have parties to get to? Or some other reason to stay in out of the cold? She hunched her shoulders and dug her hands further into her pockets. It was already hovering at freezing, with the expected lows overnight anticipated in the high teens. And now she was obsessing about the weather. Though it beat worrying about how Gabe would react to seeing her.

Ryan said he asked for her. Specifically. Did Gabe miss her?

Ryan said so but...that seemed unlikely. It wasn't as if they'd dated that long. Did it even qualify as dating? They'd gone out on dates, but dating? She stopped, moving aside to let a family pass. What was wrong with her? She was here to do a job, get a few quotes, and then she'd go home and write up the article. If the ball hadn't dropped by the time she finished, she'd put it on the TV and kiss her cats before going to bed. End of story.

Resolved, she gave a casual wave to the teen manning the gate as she passed—where was Jake tonight?—and followed the crowd toward the back of the light display where signs indicated the closing ceremony would take place. Tori slithered between family groups and couples, worming her way toward the front so she could see. All for the article, of course. She needed to be able to set the scene, so to speak.

Her gaze veered to Gabe, standing to the side of a platform that hadn't been there before. Black slacks peeked out from a thigh-length winter dress coat. He had a burgundy scarf wound around his neck and a newsboy cap on his head. Her heart raced and her lips tingled. It wasn't just his physical appearance —though that was nothing to dismiss—he radiated confidence and friendliness. He was a good man. It was just too bad he wasn't *her* good man.

He turned and spoke to someone standing beside him before hopping onto the platform and striding to the center where a podium and microphone were set up. Tori flicked on her voice recorder and pulled her wayward thoughts back in. Do the job and go home. Don't spend time regretting what might have been.

"Ladies and gentlemen, if I could have your attention please. I know everyone's freezing and ready to head off to the rest of their New Year's celebrations, so we'll make this brief. Thank you all for coming out, not just tonight, but to everyone who came throughout the month of December—I'm humbled and grateful for your generosity. Operation Mistletoe is a charity that's near and dear to my heart. Shortly after my company took off, we had a contract take us overseas to support our troops. That Christmas was one of the bleakest I've ever experienced, until OM arrived. Their mission is to bring Christmas to the men and women serving overseas—not just presents and food from home, though there's plenty of that, but the real meaning behind Christmas. The gift that is always the right size and that will never wear out or get lost. That gift is Jesus. It was through OM that I was finally willing to see how much I need Him in my life, and I'm a better man now because of Him. So every year since, I've put on this little light display and given the donations to OM to help them continue their mission. This year, I wanted to do more—to give more. I thought I needed to prove something to Jesus...but I've recently come to realize I was just trying to prove something to myself."

Tori blinked as Gabe's gaze locked with hers. A ball of heat started in her middle and spread outward.

He continued to look at her as he spoke. "In the process of figuring that out, I made one of the classic military blunders and shot the messenger. Thankfully, I only used words and it's my hope that she'll forgive me. I was wrong, Tori, to react the way I did. This—all this tonight—is because you saw me more clearly than I see myself and had the courage to put it in print. I'm sorry for how I behaved."

Tori blinked back the tears that pooled in her eyes as heat burned her cheeks. She didn't need a public apology. When she realized he—and everyone else—was still looking at her, she managed a weak smile and quick bobbing nod.

21

Gabe grinned as his muscles loosened. She forgave him. They still needed to talk things through, but there was hope. "Thanks. Without further ado, I'd like to present this enormous fake check to the Executive Director of Operation Mistletoe, William Benson."

A man with the unmistakable bearing of military service strode onto the stage and clasped Gabe's hand as he took the check. He leaned toward the mike. "I didn't realize I was standing out in the cold for a fake check or I would've sent my assistant."

The audience chuckled.

Gabe pulled a piece of paper off the giant cardboard and held it up. "The real one's paperclipped to the back. Maybe you should just tuck it in your jacket so it doesn't get lost."

William made a show of comparing the two amounts to the continued chuckles of the crowd. He folded the check into a pocket and took the mike. "Thank you, Gabe. And everyone who came out and donated. Though the main thrust of OM is Christmas, we also provide support services to military chaplains and other outreach throughout the year. Your generosity is greatly appreciated."

Gabe returned to the mike. "There's hot coffee, cocoa, and doughnuts in the snack shack. Complimentary this evening. You're welcome to wander the lights. We'll be open a while yet. And however else you choose to celebrate, have a safe and happy New Year."

His words were greeted with a smattering of applause. Gabe smiled for a few photos and once again shook William's hand. He kept one eye on Tori, though she made no move to leave. He'd half expected her to bolt as soon as they were done. Apologizing in public had put her on the spot. He needed to apologize in private, too.

It took forever to speak to everyone who lined up to admire the big check and congratulate them on their success. A handful of people wanted to know more about Jesus. Gabe and William, along with a few other volunteers, took the time to explain and answer questions. Periodically, he looked over. Tori had shifted to a bench and held a steaming cup in her hands, but she was still there. Every time their eyes locked, his heart leapt in his chest.

Finally, the last stragglers moved on and Gabe closed the distance to Tori. "Thanks for waiting. I'm sorry, Tori. So sorry."

She shook her head. "I'm sorry, too. I knew you didn't want the benefits mentioned—Angel made that clear, so please don't be angry with her. But...some of the things Geneva was trying to say made me so mad. I wanted to set the record straight. But I should've run it by you first."

He smiled, taking her hands in his. "I thought I was supposed to be the one defending your honor, not the other way around."

"I get carried away sometimes."

"Hazard of the profession?"

"Something like that."

Gabe stroked her cheek. "I missed you."

She tilted her head to the side. "It's only been a week."

"Felt like a lifetime. Don't go away again."

"Not even if you tell me to?"

"I won't."

"You've got a deal."

Gabe gazed into her eyes and caught the promise of many happy Christmases to come before he lowered his lips to hers. "Deal."

A NOTE FROM ELIZABETH...

Gabe and Tori made their way through misunderstandings and came out stronger for it on the other side. And now Tori has some happier memories to associate with Christmas and the New Year.

But the gang at Intelligence Associates isn't done yet. Rick Wentworth is on his way back to work in the office full-time. And his ex, Annabelle Elliot is working there too. Can they find a way to work together—and maybe back to love?

Read Operation Valentine today to find out.

WANT A FREE BOOK?

If you enjoyed this book and would like to read another of my books for free, you can get a free e-book simply by signing up for my newsletter on my website.

AUTHOR'S NOTE

Thank you for reading *Operation Mistletoe!* I hope that you enjoyed it! I would appreciate it if you'd help others enjoy it too by leaving a review and telling your friends about it. Any success my books have is owed to readers like you who take the time to tell others about my stories. Thank you, from the bottom of my heart.

I continue to owe a huge debt of gratitude to my husband and sons for giving me the time to write, my sister for her unflinching support and encouragement, and my critique partners Heather Gray and Jan Elder for catching all the times I use the same word six times in two paragraphs.

More than anything, I'm grateful that God continues to give me words and makes it possible for me to write them down.

I'd love to hear from you! You can connect with me on Facebook my webpage or via email. To stay current with news and occasional giveaways, please subscribe to my newsletter.

OTHER BOOKS BY ELIZABETH MADDREY

Beachfront Billionaires

Second Chance at the Seaside

Married at the Marina

Billionaire Next Door

The Billionaire's Nanny

The Billionaire's Best Friend

The Billionaire's Secret Crush

The Billionaire's Backup

The Billionaire's Teacher

The Billionaire's Wife

Postcards, A Novel

So You Want to Be a Billionaire

So You Want a Second Chance

So You Love to Hate Your Boss

So You Love Your Best Friend's Sister

So You Have My Secret Baby

So You Need a Fake Relationship

So You Forgot You Love Me

Hope Ranch Series

Hope for Christmas

Hope for Tomorrow

Hope for Love

Hope for Freedom

Hope for Family

Hope at Last

Peacock Hill Romance Series

A Heart Restored

A Heart Reclaimed

A Heart Realigned

A Heart Redirected

A Heart Rearranged

A Heart Reconsidered

Arcadia Valley Romance – Baxter Family Bakery Series

Loaves & Wishes

Muffins & Moonbeams

Cookies & Candlelight

Donuts & Daydreams

The 'Operation Romance' Series

Operation Mistletoe

Operation Valentine

Operation Fireworks

Operation Back-to-School

The 'Taste of Romance' Series

A Splash of Substance

A Pinch of Promise

A Dash of Daring

A Handful of Hope

A Tidbit of Trust

The 'Grant Us Grace' Series

Wisdom to Know

Courage to Change

Serenity to Accept

Pathway to Peace

Joint Venture

The 'Remnants' Series:

Faith Departed

Hope Deferred

Love Defined

Stand alones

Kinsale Kisses: An Irish Romance

Luna Rosa (part of A Tuscan Legacy)

Her Billionaire Benefactor (part of the Easter in Gilead series)

For the most recent listing of all my books, please visit my website.

ABOUT THE AUTHOR

USA Today bestselling author Elizabeth Maddrey is a semi-reformed computer geek and homeschooling mother of two who lives in the suburbs of Washington D.C. When she isn't writing, Elizabeth is a voracious consumer of books. She loves to write about Christians who struggle through their lives, dealing with sin and receiving God's grace on their way to their own romantic happily ever after.

[f] facebook.com/ElizabethMaddrey

[o] instagram.com/ElizabethMaddrey

[a] amazon.com/Elizabeth-Maddrey/e/B00A11QGME

[BB] bookbub.com/authors/elizabeth-maddrey

[▶] youtube.com/@ElizabethMaddreyAuthor

www.ingramcontent.com/pod-product-compliance
Lightning Source LLC
Chambersburg PA
CBHW071312130626
46556CB00004B/1577